Like A Boss

**By
Logan Chance**

*Denise —

Logan Chance*

Like A Boss

© Copyright held by Logan Chance
Published by The Brothers Chance 2016

All rights reserved. This book or any portion thereof may not be reproduced or used in any manner whatsoever without the express written permission of the publisher or author except for the use of brief quotations in a book review.

The novel is a work of fiction. Names, characters, places and plot are all either products of the author's imagination or used fictitiously. Any resemblance to actual events, locales, or persons—living or dead—is purely coincidental.

First Edition.

Content Editor: Paula Dawn
Cover Designer: Jessica Hildreth
Proofreader: Vivian Freeman

Dedication

For K.

For my Lopa.

To Batman, this one's for you. Everything I do, I succeed because you're there every step of the way. HBTY

To Obi Wan Kenobi, I wouldn't be where I am today without you. You really are one of the greats.

To The Duchess of Storms, where do I begin? You inspire me every day to write better, live harder, and love stronger.

Table of Contents

ONE

TWO

THREE

FOUR

FIVE

SIX

SEVEN

EIGHT

NINE

TEN

ELEVEN

TWELVE

THIRTEEN

FOURTEEN

FIFTEEN

ONE

THEO

Fuck, I need to get laid.

If I didn't find a woman in this bar to fuck tonight, I'd lose my mind. I was overworked and stressed beyond belief. I had no time to focus on the finer things in life. I almost forgot what the inside of a pussy felt like. Lately, I felt this champion cock I owned between my legs was just for show.

Two words:

Fuck.

That.

Nectar was packed when I stepped inside; pink and purple neon lights blinded my eyes as they swept the room. Women in leopard-print leotards hung from giant swings as the loud bass shook the floor beneath my feet. I found

Xavier, my friend, at the bar with a shot of Macallan in his hand. He passed it to me as I nodded.

With my drink in hand, I 'surveyed the land' as it were. A curvy brunette, wearing painted on jeans with red heels, smiled at me. She took a small sip of her Cosmo and the lipstick stain left behind on the glass matched her sexy shoes. She was pretty. She was absolutely fuckable. Let's be honest, most men aren't even that damn picky, but tonight I craved above average. It's why I picked Nectar—the hottest place to be on a Friday night—but while sexy, curvaceous asses and pumped up plastic tits painted the room like a surgeon's personal advertisement billboard, I wanted something closer to the liquor in my hand. I wanted a girl fresh out the damn bottle, warm in my mouth, burning on the way down, and fucking me up until I couldn't see straight. I wanted the good shit.

A raven-haired beauty, in a skimpy dress leaving nothing to the imagination, and fuck me stilettos, locked eyes with me. The hot pink-stained cheeky smile she flashed my way did nothing for me...total stage five clinger potential. *Pass.*

I nodded, and continued studying the club.

My eyes drifted to a group of girls celebrating across the bar—a bachelorette party. Penis straws in their mouths, pink boas around their necks, and falling off the barstools drunk. *Double Pass.*

"It's getting late. I might head out," Xavier, said, glancing at his gold Rolex. He grabbed his Corona by the neck and took a long pull.

"It's South Beach, this city doesn't come alive until well after midnight."

"There's not much action here tonight. But, you stay, relax, you deserve it." His eyes drifted to the crowded dance floor. "The sale is a shoo-in; you'll be the proud owner of the Bearded Goat within a few months."

"Thanks, man. Yeah, it's been stressful as fuck these past few days." I lifted my glass and took a sip, letting the liquor ease the tension in my shoulders.

He laughed, chugging his beer, and spun in his seat to slam the empty bottle on the bar.

"I think I got the brunt of your stress." Xavier, also my lawyer, had been busy working his ass off for me. He scoured over paperwork and legal documents making sure I got the best deal possible.

"Fuck you, buddy. It's my ass on the line here. First thing I'm doing with the bar is changing the fucking name." I threw some cash to the bartender and returned my attention back to him. "Bearded Goat, really? Why not call it the lamest bar in Miami?"

"Think about it, one day you can have a place just like this." He lifted his arms, pointing to the bright lights of Nectar that showcased the energy of the nightclub.

I grinned, turning to rest my elbows against the bar. "I'm sure my place will be a hell of a lot better." My eyes traveled around as I scoped the joint once more. Yeah, my club would be much nicer. I could see it all now. I would soon own South Beach. How hard could running a bar be? I'd never failed at anything I'd gone after before, and this time wouldn't be any fucking different.

"On second thought," Xavier said, eyes trained on the party of pink madness a few yards away,

"I'm going to join the action over there."

I nodded, and watched him stalk over to make his play on one of the bachelorettes from the party. She offered him a drink from her penis straw and laughed when he grabbed it and directed it back to her mouth, shaking his head. I grinned—what an idiot.

"Hi...what's your name?" a drunk plastic blonde asked, as she slid onto the stool next to me, arms hanging around my neck. Her platinum hair hung straight and fell past her tits. She leaned in closer, giving me a glimpse straight down her plum-colored, v-neck dress to her manufactured cleavage.

"Theo." I threw back my whiskey, and signaled the bartender for another before turning to face her.

Her ass left the seat and she stepped between my long legs, her fingers running up the length of my red tie. "I'm

Ashley." Her breathy words fanned across my lips as she lifted her hand to run it through my beard. "I've never seen you around. Do you *come* here a lot?" she asked, her voice thick as honey, seduction dripping off her tongue.

My brown eyes focused on the gigantic rock on her finger before removing her hand from my face. "No." I'd been coming here for the past week, to check out the competition for my newest acquisition, but tonight I needed release and this girl wasn't the one.

I stood, giving her a tight smile, before making my way to the other end of the neon lit bar.

I squeezed my tall frame to an empty stool and signaled the bartender. "Whiskey," I called out to her.

She glanced my way, locking eyes with mine. A brief nod and a slight smile was all she gave me before she turned and slammed a few bottles back in the well. The sexy bartender finally slid her ass over and my eyes narrowed on her as she poured the whiskey in a glass. Her shimmery hair clearly wasn't hers. The wig on her head matched her silver bikini top, which barely contained her full breasts. The skinny strings strained, as if at any moment they would snap, letting her tits fall free. A silver short skirt hugged the curve of her ass as she turned to pour a few shots for the bride-to-be.

The few times I'd been here, I'd never seen this girl. I'd remember a face like hers, even in the dark. My eyes scanned her flawless features. She wasn't hard and overworked like some of these girls. She hadn't allowed a scalpel to redraw the map of who she was designed to be. And she sure as shit wasn't shy about showing it off. My dick stiffened. That hunger to claim and guzzle down the good shit surged. And I'm not talking about fucking whiskey, either. I wanted her.

Nights like these were sort of like the Sabbath to me, a holy day to worship my most favorite idol, a woman's sweet body. This woman with silver hair and spilling breasts was in need of worship and I had every intention of fucking her like the goddess she was. I'd spend many nights doing just that, but…

first, I had to get her attention.

Again.

After a few minutes, I decided to use the secret super power I owned. It would require the use of a couple of ladies with penis straws in their mouths. When she finally returned to ask if I wanted another, I leaned in, talking close to her ear over the loud music.

 My scruffy cheek whispered across her smooth skin. "As a father, I have to beg you to please cut those girls off." I nodded in the direction of the bachelorette party. Her eyes flitted to them and then back to me. "If it were my little Lucy, I'd be devastated to know they'd be driving home like that." Daddy role never failed me before.

"Relax," she shot back. "They have a limo waiting in the lot. *Daddy Dearest.*"

I smiled at her and leaned back in. "Just so you know, you're the hottest girl in this whole fucking place."

"Just so *you* know," she said, touching my shoulder this time, "you're the millionth guy who has said that tonight."

I pulled back, palms splayed on the bar as I met her eyes. "But there's a difference—you want to know what it is?"

She shrugged, causing her tits to squeeze together. I grabbed my empty glass and held it up to her, leaning in close again, not breaking eye contact. "I'm the only fucker in here who will say *please.*"

"Fuck," I groaned, breaking from the lips of the silver goddess. Tongues twisting, mouths sucking, her sexy moans were pulling me under. "You want to do this here?"

With a strong grip around her waist, I pulled her even closer, grinding my cock against her.

"You have to live a little," she said as she pushed away and ran toward the shoreline.

The waves crashed as I strolled along with my hands in my pockets, fascinated by her.

Her silver wig and long legs held the moon's glow as she laughed. Her toes dipped into the salty ocean and as I watched—my arousal deepened.

I took a long breath as I saw her dance in the moonlight. Fucking hot, the way her ass shook, the way she grooved to a rhythm playing along in her mind. I wanted to hear it too.

I'd been overworked for so long, and she made me feel like I'd been set free.

She shimmied over, her arms landing around my neck as I gazed into her glitter-shadowed eyes. "Dance with me."

We swayed and rocked into one another as I caressed the dip of her spine with one hand. "Your name, what is it?"

"Penelope."

Penelope. It rolled along my tongue as I said it aloud.

"Are you going to tell me yours or do I have to guess?"

"Take your best shot," I egged her on.

She placed a finger to her suckable lips, gazing skyward before returning her copper eyes to mine. "I don't know. Maybe Frank. You look like a Frank."

I cocked a brow. "Do I? No, not Frank. Name's Theo."

"Ah...Theo...I see now."

I raised a brow. "See what?"

"Your name...I see how you managed to get me out here. You had God on your side." She laughed, moving closer. "Theo means God given." Her eyes met mine with intensity. "Feeling like a saint or a sinner tonight, Theo?"

"Oh, definitely a fucking sinner," I said, grabbing her, "and worshipping, namely, you."

Where can I fuck this girl, already? The beach—too sandy. The ocean—too wet.

A lifeguard station sat off in the distance and I was already pulling Penelope in that direction.

"Get your sexy ass up there." I grabbed a handful as she stepped her first foot in the rung of the ladder.

"Race you to the top," she said, laughing as she glanced down to me.

Damn, this sexy temptress teased me. A snap decision and I took off running toward another staircase off to the left.

I'd get to the top before her if my life depended on it.

A sexy smirk, fingers playing with the strands of her shimmery top, and a wicked gleam in her eyes awaited me when I reached the large deck.

"Damn, you're quick," I breathed out fast.

"Not quick at everything." The way she batted her fake eyelashes made my heart beat faster.

"Yeah, I like to take things nice and slow, too." I grabbed the handrails, leaning over slightly as I gradually made my way to her.

"Just the way I like it," she paused as I stalked even closer. "Well, sometimes." She winked as I reached her. My hands moved to the sides of her face, drawing her in, my lips capturing hers once again.

The feel of her tongue tracing along mine and my cock sprang to life. Her sexy curves pressed against me as I guided her back toward the lifeguard chair.

A soft summer breeze, a light touch of air, a slight shiver of Penelope's body had me holding on tighter.

Breaking the kiss, I glanced over her, memorizing the way she sparkled with the backdrop of the ocean behind her.

"You're stunning," I whispered across her glittery skin.

She blushed, even with the heavy makeup, before she ran her hand along the front of my pants gripping my hardness underneath.

"Yeah, stroke my cock," I growled against her silver wig, rocking my hips into her hand. Her mouth sucked my neck as my fingers worked the ties of her bikini top, freeing her tits for me to see.

Edging her closer to the seat, I ran my hand over her heightened nipple—squeezing, tugging, and then sucking it with my hungry mouth. She whimpered, running her fingers through my hair, pulling it roughly.

I was in control now, and I wanted her to know it.

"Where do you want me to touch you?" I asked as she gazed with a fire in her eyes.

"Everywhere," she whispered.

I would get her to say what I wanted to hear.

Lightly, I traced a finger down her neck, feeling her pulse quicken as she moaned. "Here?"

"Yeah," was her breathy reply.

My finger traveled down through the valley of her cleavage. I groaned feeling the soft skin of each tit as they pressed against me. "Here?"

She sighed heavily. "Yes, please." Her back arched off the wood railing as she tried to press her body further into my eager touch.

I slid my finger to the right and grazed over her hardened nipple and snapped it gently between my thumb and forefinger. "Here?"

"Oh God, yes."

My lips lifted, my hand cupping her perfect breast as I etched the outline of her stomach. I slid further down until I reached her leg and brought it to rest on my hip. My fingers traced under her silver skirt, squeezing her ass. "Here?"

"Yes, yes."

The lace of her panties was rough on my finger as I ran it underneath, feeling her wetness. "Here?"

With a sharp inhale, she answered, "Fuck, yes."

My finger slipped inside her and her breathing sped up when I added a second. "Is this where you want me to touch you?"

She rocked her hips as I sucked along her collarbone. "Yes, don't stop," she begged.

"Tell me, tell me you want me to touch your pussy."

"I want you to touch my pussy," she echoed.

"Louder."

She spoke up and I drowned out her admission with my mouth on her lips. I sucked down her words as my fingers picked up their rhythm.

Her silver-coated nails dug into my back, clawing at the material of my Oxford shirt. "Tell me you want me to fuck you," I demanded, my voice husky with greed to claim every god damn inch of her.

Eyes gleaming in the moonlight, she repeated my words.

I pulled my coated fingers from her and smeared the wetness across her full lips. "Lick your lips for me."

Her sparkling lashes fanned across her cheeks as she closed her eyes and her pink tongue licked along the curve of her lips, savoring herself. *Goddamn, this girl.*

I slid my fingers inside her and soaked them once more. I lifted my hand again. "Open, Penelope, taste yourself." Her eyes never wavered from mine as her pouty lips pursed around my finger. My mind filled with images of what they would look like around my hardening cock.

"Fuck, that's right," I bit out. "See how sweet you taste? I want to taste it too. I want to kiss you with the flavor of your pussy in our mouths."

Smashing my lips to hers, starved to taste every part of her, I devoured what she offered. A low, gravelly sound rumbled in the back of my throat. *So fucking good.*

I could come from the taste alone.

"Turn around," I commanded. She complied as I unzipped my pants, freeing myself.

"Take off your panties." She glanced over her shoulder and lowered them down her long legs. I watched with needy eyes as the lace fell to the weathered boards beneath our feet.

She bent over, hands on the arms of the chair, baring her pussy for me to see.

Damn, she was gorgeous. I was one lucky son-of-a-bitch tonight.

The condom was on my cock in record time and I reached out feeling along her wet pussy. I growled; she was fucking soaked.

I ran the tip of my heavy dick along her seam, toying with her clit. Her head fell back in ecstasy. "Fuck me, Theo. Fuck me like you own me."

"Fuck yeah, are you ready for me to worship you?"

"Yes, yes. Please."

With desperation I slammed inside her. *Jesus.* Jaw clenched, my eyes closed and I gripped her hips as the feel of her insanely hot pussy overcame my senses. Dripping and sweet—oh so fucking sweet. I pumped, and pushed deeper inside her, as she writhed and bucked with me.

I trailed a hand up her back, feeling her tender skin beneath my fingers. When I reached her neck, I spread them around her throat and nipped along her earlobe. "Fuck, it feels so good."

Her wet, tight cunt made my fingers race to touch her clit. I snapped it within my fingers as she cried out a string of unintelligible words.

We screwed like only two strangers on a deserted beach could, rough and wild. She moaned loudly as I went deeper and deeper, harder and fucking harder. My mind was sewn with lust, yearning and craving more from this silver temptress. I needed to feel her come on my cock.

With my focus solely on her pleasure, my fingers tightened around her throat as I kissed and licked up the nape of her neck. When I brushed the wig aside to find more skin,

I noticed a small tattoo. Tracing my thumb along the tiny turtle of ink, I slowed for a beat before resuming my rigorous tempo.

She was sexy as fuck and I didn't want it to end.

She was definitely the good shit. Hell, she was fucking better than that.

My thumb circled around her clit as I pressed against it. "Penelope, your pussy... so good."

I pumped inside—*fuck yeah, she's hot.*

I went harder—*Oh damn.*

I plunged further—*her pussy. Oh God.*

She was like magic, making me see my orgasm coming along the skyline. Soon it would slam into her with such force I'd need both hands to hold me up when it was all over.

She pushed her ass further against me, meeting my punishing strokes. I licked along her soft skin and breathed in the scent of coconut, feeling her tighten around me.

"Oh God, I feel you. Damn."

"I'm coming," she screamed.

The most heavenly of sounds; her voice like an angel singing only for me.

I slapped her ass, rugged and harsh, as she climaxed over and over. I kept pounding, enjoying the feeling of her clamping down around me.

My climax built as I kissed along her tattoo once more.

"You're beautiful," I murmured, as the need to come overpowered me.

I couldn't contain it any longer and the beast inside unleashed. Untamed, I came with such force I wouldn't have survived if her body didn't grip mine.

I kissed the turtle tattoo once as I slid out.

The next morning, I awoke to the sun beating down on me. Seagulls flew high in the clear, blue sky and the dried out wooden boards under my head made my skull ache. A man in yellow swim trunks stared down at me as I took my time sitting up.

"Rough night?" he asked.

"Yeah," I grumbled, searching for Penelope.

She was nowhere to be found.

That very night I went back to Nectar, with the lights dancing around the club and the music blaring, it felt very reminiscent of the night before.

I went directly to the bar, searching for the silver siren whose body was a work of art.

A burly bartender tossed bottles in the air as women around the bar cheered. After he finished, his attention landed on me.

"What can I get you to drink, man?"

"Is Penelope working?" I asked over the loud music.

Confused, he shook his head back and forth. "No one works here by that name."

"Are you sure? *Penelope.*" I put an extra emphasis on her name, saying it loud and clear.

"No, she doesn't work here. Sorry dude."

I stepped away from the bar with a sinking feeling coming over me. I searched the club for a while before making my way home.

For weeks I wondered about her, who was she? I sometimes thought I saw her pass by me on Collins Ave. Other days, I swore I saw her in the tourist shops along Ocean Drive. Each day she haunted my thoughts as I longed to be inside her once more.

TWO

PENNY

"Come on my cock, Penelope." He pulled me closer as my orgasm rolled through my body over and over.

My eyes flew open. Another dreamgasm. Panting, my pulse racing, I tried to return my breathing back to normal as I pulled the covers up higher over my head. Trembling, I blew out a shaky breath and stretched my body along the cool cotton sheets trying desperately to return back to sleep, back to the dream I had every night for the past few months.

Silver wig, ocean view and one of the greatest nights, ever. Theo. His name fit him perfectly; he fucked like a God. Our night meant everything to me, until I left the gorgeous stranger. I'd wanted to stay with him until he woke, but an urgent text from my boss of Nectar put a damper on those plans. I took one last look at the sexy man and watched the rise and fall of his perfectly cut, tanned chest as the sun turned the darkened sky light-blue and pink. His full lips were slightly parted as he slept soundly beside me. I brushed a soft kiss against them and rushed off to Nectar.

My manager, and his hideous toupee falling off to the left side more than the right, waited with fuming red cheeks. I'd been fired right then for not getting permission to leave, even though I made sure Garcia watched the bar for me. No amount of pleading on my part would get him to change his mind.

Back then, I felt as if I'd never find another gig paying as much as Nectar. The regret about losing a job for something so foolish entered my mind many times, but I quickly squashed it when I remembered how magical the night was. I needed work though. South Beach was competitive as hell. Sure, I could make bank in one night, but try finding *the* job. I'd finally lucked out getting hired at The Bearded Goat, a tiki-style bar close to the beach. Half indoors, half-out, it was a laid back, chill job.

"What's that far off look you have?" Margo, my roommate, asked, making her way into my room and sitting on the orange-flowered comforter on my bed.

I kicked back the covers and ran my hands through my long, sun-kissed hair. "I dreamt about sexy stranger again." Crossing to the white oak dresser, I opened my drawer and peered inside.

Her perfectly arched brows rose. "Oh, Lord of the O's?"

I laughed, slipping on the just shy of ridiculous Bearded Goat tank. It was a far cry from what I barely wore at Nectar. "Yeah him," I said, grabbing a pair of jean shorts and sliding them up my legs. "Did I tell you his name meant God given? Well, God definitely gave and kept on giving. If you know what I mean."

"Yes, I know, I know. He was a sex God," she said, laughing.

"Among other things." I laughed along with her as I thought about Theo once more. Something about him drew me to him. I'd never left the bar with a customer, let alone had sex with one in the middle of a shift.

"But, you have Dex now," she said, pulling a plump pillow into her lap. "You're happy with him, right?"

"Yeah, I'm glad I met Dex, of course. I just hate how he works all the time." And how different he seemed since he left.

"Things are okay between the two of you, right?" Her eyes grew serious as she gazed at me.

"Yeah, sure." I brushed off her question. "I sometimes wonder what would have happened if I stayed with Lord of the O's." I sighed and sat down on the bed next to her.

"Well for starters you wouldn't have met Dex," she said, giving my knee a nudge with hers.

"Well, true." My fingers played with the hem of my shorts before my eyes slid to hers. "Dex is great don't get me wrong, I just wonder sometimes."

"Oh Penny, don't feel guilty. It was only a dream. It's normal to wonder about the greatest sex of your life from time to time." Her laughter filled the sunny room as I slapped her lightly on the arm.

"I never said he was the greatest sex I ever had."

"Oh please, you haven't stopped talking about him for months, even after you met Dex."

I blushed. She had a point. "You may be right." I laughed.

"So, today's the big day, right?" Margo's question brought me back to the dread I felt.

I sighed, rising from the bed. "Yeah, from what I hear this guy's like some hot-shot real estate guru. So, this should be interesting." I swept my long hair off my shoulders and threw it into a low ponytail.

"Has he ever owned a bar before?"

"I'm sure he's never worked hard a day in his life." I thought about my father, and knew this hot-shot was probably exactly like him, relentless how everything revolved around money. I applied my lip gloss and pursed my lips together.

"I'm sure. So, any hot plans with Dex tonight?" Her long blonde hair flowed down her back as she ran her fingers through it, playing with the ends.

"Truth is, I haven't heard from him in a few days. He's on a 'business trip'," I raised my fingers to signal the air quotes, "and who knows what he's doing."

"Have you tried calling him?"

I shot her a look, with a raised brow. "What do you think?"

"I'm sure he'll call. You two haven't been dating long. He probably needs a good ass-kicking to get his head on straight." She laughed but I didn't find her words very funny.

It bugged me he hadn't called—who doesn't have time to call their girlfriend? Although I didn't really feel much like a girlfriend anymore.

"What does Richie think about the place getting bought out?" She rose from the bed and smoothed the wrinkles out of the skirt of her pink sundress.

"Oh, you know Richie, he only thinks about retiring." I stuffed my gloss and phone into my red stylish purse. "I hope he does as he promised before he leaves."

"About putting in a good word for you for bar manager?" Margo's baby blue eyes grew curious as she waited for my answer.

"Yeah. I should get going or I'll be late. Have fun at the gym." I grabbed my keys and headed for the door as Margo called my name.

"Penny, don't worry about Dex. I can see how much he likes you. I'm sure he'll call, maybe he's really busy," she said.

I sighed and threw my bag over my shoulder. I knew he was busy. I knew he had important meetings. Working for a land developer left him little time for phone calls to his girlfriend, I guessed.

"Before you go, do you think I should wear the pink yoga pants or the black? Which ones make my ass look hotter?"

I shook my head, laughing.

"Pink," I yelled over my shoulder as I rushed down the hallway.

The breeze off the ocean only helped ward off the heat a little. I hoped the first thing this new owner would do is put in large oscillating fans. They would fit nicely in the large space between the top of the tiki roof and the bar.

In my off time I priced the fans and knew they would be cheap and easy to install, so I hoped he would be open for suggestions.

The traffic on the way to work was heavy. Of course it was. It figured on the day I'd meet the new boss everyone in Miami would decide to take the same route as me. I glanced down at the built-in clock to check to see if I would be late.

"Go,'' I mumbled to the car in front of me.

I rushed through a yellow light at the moment it turned red.

Flashing blue and red lights followed me through the intersection and I silently cursed myself. *Shit.*

Being late to meet the new boss wasn't something I wanted. How bad would it look going in there and saying, 'Hi, nice to meet you. Sorry I'm late. Can we get big fans? I'm hot.'

Glancing in the rearview mirror, I watched as the big, burly officer approached my driver's side window. I lowered it and grabbed my purse, pulling out my license.

"Ma'am, do you know why I pulled you over?"

I sat there quiet for a moment, thinking. This felt like a test. I chewed my lip debating on whether to lie. Should I try the waterworks to get out of a ticket? Should I lower my tank and show him my cleavage? With his pinched face, he didn't look like he would appreciate my assets.

I decided on honesty. "Yes, sir."

"License and registration."

I nodded and gave him a tight smile before I handed over the paperwork. "Would you mind if I called my work to let them know I'm running late?"

The cop nodded and I dialed the number.

"Fiona, it's Penny. I got pulled over by a cop. I might be a few minutes late." With the pace of how slow the cop moved it appeared I would be later than a minute or two. More like half an hour at his snail's pace.

Hurry up please.

"Ok, get here as soon as possible. Mr. Sullivan is already here. And you'll never believe it, Richie quit. Said he didn't want to work for a new owner."

Great, just what I wanted to hear. I hung up, tossing my phone in my handbag as the cop ran my license.

My mind reeled with news of Richie, who would manage the bar now? I wanted to.

I tapped the steering wheel hoping the movement would hurry him along. It didn't. I blew my wispy bangs from my eyes as I tapped my foot in rhythm to my hyper fingers.

My body heated as the warm air drifted into the lowered window of my little red Jetta causing a tiny bead of sweat to trickle down between my breasts.

My eyes drifted to the clock again. The Bearded Goat would be opening in twenty minutes. I ran a mental checklist through my mind as I thought of the quickest way to handle the workload.

After what seemed like hours, Officer Snail finally returned my paperwork and sent me on my way with a ticket for running the red light. *Asshole.*

Getting to work ten minutes before opening didn't leave me much time and it certainly didn't give off the best first impression I hoped for. Ever since I heard about the buyout and new owner, I was upset—with myself mostly. Mainly because I planned on speaking to Richie about giving me more responsibilities at the bar. At Nectar I was head bartender, and even sometimes a shift leader, taking care of inventory and scheduling. I was more than qualified and knew all the regulars by name. The Bearded Goat needed an overhaul, and I knew what to do to turn it into the money maker it should be. Just because I was new at *this* bar didn't mean I was new to the industry. I knew my fucking shit.

Instead of speaking to Richie, I chickened out while waiting for the ideal moment, which was like waiting for rain in a desert. Funny thing, there never was a perfect time and if you waited for it, then you'd be left waiting an eternity. My whole life I waited for the perfect moment, you know, the one where your whole life falls into place. I wanted more than anything to be a success without my father's help, but all I ever had was a lifetime of regrets, it seemed. Talking to Richie should have been easy, but instead I let it slip away. Now, with a new owner, who apparently knew nothing of the industry, according to the rumor mill, I worried I wouldn't get the opportunity again.

When I finally got to work, I ran to the heavy wooden door of the Bearded Goat and swung it open. The coast was clear except for a few cocktail servers setting up the seating area along the back deck. Making haste, I threw my bag behind the bar and assessed exactly what needed to be done before opening.

Everything.

Hustling my ass from front of the house to back of the house, I set everything up as the first customers entered through the doors. My bangs stuck to my forehead from the early morning humidity in the air, and a few soft waves escaped my ponytail.

"Penny, check the Heineken tap, it was running low yesterday," Seth said from across the bar before heading back into the kitchen.

Behind the bar, I pulled on the brass handle of the spigot. Foam overflowed and I quickly slammed it off. The Goat offered thirty beers on tap, so when a keg went empty I became a pro at changing them in a second.

Cold air blew in a rush over me when I entered the cooler and found the new Heineken keg wasn't where it should be. As I tried rolling it over to the spigot, I realized it was pointless, it wouldn't even budge. Determined, I nearly threw my back out as I tried again, grunting slightly as I made little progress.

As I bent over trying to finagle the keg, a shadow blocked the bright light from the kitchen shining into the dimly lit space.

I glanced over my shoulder, not really noticing who walked in, only noticing how the door was quickly closing behind him. "Hey," I called out, "don't let the door…" The door slammed, locking us both inside. "shut," my voice trailed off.

"What?" the stranger asked, turning to face me, but I was already racing toward the door.

"The door is locked now, genius." I brushed past his tall frame and jiggled the handle. I dropped my forehead to the cold metal and let out a sigh.

"Well, why didn't you tell me?"

"Really?" I asked, glancing over my shoulder up at him. If looks could kill, he'd be dead.

His gaze met mine for the first time since our predicament and a shiver coursed through me. I didn't know if it was from the cold of the cooler, or his eyes. *His eyes.*

I'd seen those before, deep and dark, holding mine months ago as he owned my body in the moonlight.

It was him. Theo from the beach.

Oh God. Theo.

The Lord of my O's.

"You should have a sign or something on the wall about the door locking. Why didn't you tell me when I came in?" His deep voice brought me back from my memories and it took a moment to register his question. "Are you going to answer me?"

My eyes met his harsh stare and it dawned on me. The Lord of my O's didn't recognize me.

THREE

THEO

Whoa, who the fuck is she?

Normally being locked in a cooler with a girl would be a good excuse for a chance to fuck. But, I was the boss now. I couldn't screw my employees. Even if they were as hot as her. Hell, this little vixen with the copper eyes and cute, petite figure would certainly find her way into my personal spank bank. But, that's as far as she'd ever get with me.

Who made a door which locked from the inside, anyways? Dumbest thing I ever heard.

Her eyes were wide as she stared at me. She looked like she saw a ghost. What the fuck was she thinking? And why did I care?

This wasn't supposed to happen. Finding my employees irresistible wasn't what I should be focusing on.

Getting the fuck out of here as quickly as possible before my cock got rock solid is what I should I be focused on.

This girl was trouble. I already knew it.

Turning to face me, she rested her back against the cooler door. "I did tell you." Crossing her arms, she slanted her head at me, waiting. "Besides, who doesn't know to leave the door open?"

Unbelievable. I stood with my arms crossed over my chest, looking down at her. "Are you blaming me?" I asked, drawing my brows together. "This isn't my fault. There should be a sign or something."

She laughed. "A sign? What bar uses a sign? It's common knowledge."

"Common knowledge? Says who? You?" Was this girl for real? What if we got locked in here during a busy Saturday night? She was a bit sassy, and it was really getting on my nerves.

"No, not *me*," she said, pushing off of the door, "Anyone who ever worked a day in a bar knows."

My jaw ticked as I narrowed my eyes, was I that obvious? Sure, I'd never worked in a bar before, but come on, how hard could it be? "I'm sure other bars have a sign, or some other way to know the door locks. What kind of company makes a cooler that locks from the inside? It's stupid," I said.

"All companies. I guess they want to trap people inside for the hell of it."

"Yeah well, I'm making a call." I reached into my pocket and pulled out my phone.

I held the phone in the air watching the bars disappear. Fuck, no signal.

"What's wrong, hotshot?"

I closed my eyes briefly, lifting my chin toward the ceiling before finally glancing back at her. "I have no service."

"I could have told you that," she said as she brushed past me.

"Well, if you're so smart, how do we get out of here?" I asked, turning to face her, watching as she plunked her curvy ass down on a keg, her tits bouncing as she sat. The tank she wore had a huge caricature of a bearded goat drinking a beer and I cracked a smile as I glared at it. The way the shirt was designed made her nipple look like it was in his open mouth, it was bizarre.

"We wait for someone to open the door." She ran her hands briskly up and down her arms.

"What if no one comes?" I taunted.

Her eyes widened in mock horror. "Well, I guess we freeze to death." She smiled and all I could think was, *oh fuck she's pretty.*

"Funny," I said, sliding my phone back in my pocket. "What's your name?" The white cotton of my shirt pulled tightly across my arms.

"Penny. Let me guess, you must be the new owner. The hot-shot real estate guy?"

"Hot shot?" I grazed my teeth along my lower lip before releasing it. "That's the second time you've called me hot-shot. You also called me genius. So, I guess you can call me hot-shot genius if you like, or Theo Sullivan." I closed the distance between us and leaned in. I needed to remind myself more than her nothing would ever happen between us. "Your boss."

FOUR

PENNY

The Lord of My O's was my new boss?

My body froze, and my jaw dropped as his stern stare held me captive. His hair, once neat and close cut, was now an ink-black, tousled mess on top of his head. And those lips, framed by a close-cut beard, which grazed along my shoulder as he used them to trace over me, were currently frowning at me. Memories of our chance encounter flooded my mind as I remembered his strong, muscled arms holding me close. Silently, I seethed. Was I unmemorable? Maybe I should tell him. My make-up must have been really caked on, and the wig must have done the trick, because this guy had no clue who I was. And now I worked for him. My hands stilled on my arms. Realization set in; my boss. What were the chances he would keep me around after he knew who I was? I couldn't imagine he would feel comfortable working with me everyday after the intimacy we shared. This was bad, I didn't want him to recognize me now. I couldn't lose this job. He gazed over my hardened nipples from the chill of the cooler. I crossed my arms over my chest, paranoid he would know my tits were from the night we shared. His eyes shot back up to mine, and I waited for recognition to light his thick-lashed, dark eyes. It didn't. A tinge of hurt crept in. I understood he didn't recognize who I was, but knowing his charming act I fell for was one he'd probably rehearsed and played out many times before stung. *What a player.*

I stood abruptly and he retreated from my space.

"Since we're stuck in here, would you mind helping me lift the keg so I can change the tap spigot?"

"Ok, sure. Since we have a little free time. I didn't think I'd be working hard on my first day, though," he said.

"What's wrong, afraid of a little hard work?"

He walked closer, towering over me. The way he gazed down on me made my body erupt with goosebumps, more so than the air of the cooler. My traitorous body pulsed and thrummed deep inside and my legs shook slightly. I noticed a tiny faint scar slashing through the edge of his left dark brow. *Oh shit, he's so good looking. How could I get through this every day?*

"I've never been afraid of anything in my life. Where's the keg?" he asked with a slight bit of teasing in his voice.

"There," I pointed, motioning toward the Heineken keg I attempted to move earlier.

He grabbed the keg, moving it over with little effort and brought it closer to the coupler.

His warm hand brushed against mine as we tried to get the spigot hooked up, and I didn't want to be touching him. Touching would lead to remembering. Deflated, I made a decision to never tell him about our one night on the beach, which obviously meant more to me than him. I quickly backed away, sliding my hand into the pocket of my shorts. A few moments later the door swung open.

Theo stalked out, not even taking a second glance my way.

What the hell? New owner. Fuck my life.

"Penny," Theo called from behind me. "Come join us on the patio."

A few of the employees gathered at a table on the deck as Theo instructed. I made my way over and took a seat next to Fiona.

"What's this?" I whispered next to her ear.

"Not sure." She shrugged her tanned shoulders. "He wanted to talk to all of us."

"I'm glad I could get a few of you together." Our attention turned to Theo as he spoke. "I wanted to introduce myself. I'm Theo Sullivan, the new owner." His hands grasped an empty wicker chair in front of him, and I fidgeted in my seat remembering the way they trailed over my body. "I know it's a big shock to everyone about Richard quitting this morning. It's definitely something I wasn't expecting, but let's move forward. Until he's replaced, I'll be filling in for him."

My brow furrowed and we all glanced around at each other. Maybe it was shock, maybe we were curious, either way, we were riveted.

"Any questions?" he asked.

No one spoke.

He smiled and my stomach did a little flip at the boyish grin. "Ok, good. Now let's get back to work. If anyone knows of anyone looking for a management job," he laughed, slightly, "send them my way." He raked his fingers through his dark hair as we all slowly rose from our seats.

This was my moment, my opening to take the leap. I wanted the management job and I was determined to get it. I stepped away from the chair, eyes trained on Theo and took a deep breath.

Nerves churned in my stomach, of course, but I hid them with the biggest smile I could muster in the moment. "Hello, again, Mr. Sullivan."

"Hi, Penny, what can I do for you?" he asked.

"I was wondering about the management job. I'd like to apply."

He raked his eyes over my clothes, and I felt underdressed. With his grey dress slacks, and white button down, I felt I should be wearing a pencil skirt and silk blouse to apply. Maybe this was a bad idea.

"I'm kind of looking for someone different." He unbuttoned the top button of his shirt, tugging his tie loose. "Man, it's hot."

My disbelieving eyes grew at the audacity he would discount me so easily. He didn't even give me an opportunity to list my qualifications.

I squared my shoulders and raised my chin. "Well, Richie said he thought I'd be a good fit for management."

"Penny, can I ask you a question?"

"Sure." I saw a seagull land off the back deck as my eyes returned to Theo and I kind of hoped it would shit on his head.

"You were late today, are you always late to work?"

Damn. I gazed at him with what I hoped was a doe-eyed expression as I tried to figure out what to say.

This wasn't going at all as planned, but I tried to make the best of the situation. Always the optimist, or so I pretended. "No sir, I'm never late. Most days I'm early. I work hard, and I'm always the first person called when they need a shift covered. But today I was pulled over."

"So you want to be the boss, huh?" His eyes bore into mine as I shifted on my feet. "I would start by being on time for work in the future. Maybe leave your house earlier, so you aren't speeding."

"Yes, sir," I said, giving him a nod before turning away.

An older woman with a bright orange and green moo moo dress called me over, and I was happy to escape him.

I conversed with her as Theo walked around glancing at different things. He never let go of the clipboard in his hands, taking notes every so often with a pen he perched behind his ear.

Sexiness oozed from him. It was hard to believe this cocky as hell man was the same one from the beach.

By the next day, it was obvious he didn't know the first thing about running a bar. On Wednesday, he wanted me to alphabetize the liquor bottles, which, of course, made me laugh in his face. I thought he was joking. He wasn't. I told him no functioning bar could run that way. Bottles were displayed according to well, call, and brand names. He listened stone faced as I explained how the phrase 'top shelf' actually meant the bottles on the top shelf were better quality, as well as more expensive. It applied in all bars, not because they're organized alphabetically.

When he wasn't walking around with his clipboard, endlessly taking notes, he spent most of his time on the phone, or joking with other employees. They appeared to love him. I felt like I was the only one concerned our new owner knew little to nothing about the industry. I wanted the management position, and one way or another I would show him I was the best person for the job. My resolve strengthened to never tell him who I was. He didn't make it easy though. Watching how he would nibble on the end of a pen, or run it across his lips, when he thought about a new ridiculous idea for the bar, made me want to strangle his neck while I kissed him.

By Thursday, I was sure he lost his mind when he wanted all of us to stop what we were doing to acknowledge each time a guest entered or left the establishment with a 'hello' or a 'goodbye.' Sure, it was a fun idea in theory, but it was impractical.

Friday came and Theo still had no clue, but I gave him one thing—he wasn't giving up. He had a big heart, which was evidenced by how he let some of the older locals tell him story after story about the 'good ol' days.' He would lean on the bar, his dark eyes lighting with laughter, as he listened. He worked hard, I could begrudgingly admit, even though the work he did was all wrong.

"What do you think?" Fiona asked as she leaned against the bar.

"Of?"

"Mr. Sullivan. Too bad he's our boss and not a customer. I'd flirt my ass off with him. So damn handsome." She closed her eyes for a moment and made an "Mm" sound.

"I don't think he'll last. So maybe you'll get lucky." Vomit. I wanted to vomit as I played with the top of a Vodka bottle in the well by my side.

"Apparently he has a ton of great ideas." Her dark hair flew around her face as a breeze swept in. "Not that we've seen any yet." She smiled.

"Yeah, I don't think this guy would know a good idea if it slapped him in his bearded face. He's just another pompous asshole, playing bar owner, and I'm sure he'll run this place into the ground." My cheeks heated, my heart pumping, maybe I was being unfair, but so was he. Two more times I approached him about the management position and both times he shot me down.

"If he runs it into the ground then I guess it's time to start looking for another job." She winked as she walked away. The problem was I didn't want a new job; I liked the Goat.

My eyes traveled to the spacious patio with its more than half empty wooden seats. People would rather spend their days at the Clevelander or The Mango Tropical Cafe than to come here. A gentle ocean breeze stirred the loose strands of hair escaping my ponytail as I stood behind the bar watching the waves crash in the distance.

"And she wants to be manager." I jumped at the sound of Theo's weighty voice behind me. He motioned to an empty lounger with his head. "Would you like to take a nap, *Boss*?" he quipped.

My eyes widened and I bit back a retort. "As you can see, we have no customers to take care of."

"Time to lean," he pulled a bar towel from his shoulder, "Time to clean*. Boss."* He motioned to the bar he knew damn well I kept impeccably clean as I gazed at his reflection in the mirror.

"I've already cleaned the bar. You know I always keep it in order. You want me to do it again?" I challenged.

"Yes. Yes, I would."

"Why don't you say *please*." I seethed, wanting to remind him of our night together, but he still didn't catch my implied meaning.

The Lord Of My O's could fuck off.

FIVE

THEO

Say please, my ass.

Listening to them talk about me—the way they thought I would run this bar into the ground—pissed me the fuck off. Pompous asshole? Who me? They didn't know what the fuck they were talking about.

I wasn't born yesterday and I worked hard for everything I had. There was no silver spoon in my mouth when I was born, and I never failed at anything I ever set out to do before in my whole goddamn life—and that was a fact.

I tugged at my tie as the heat coursing through my agitated veins compounded.

The previous owner told me business was good, and even showed me his books. Glancing around at the empty bar area, I questioned if he fudged the numbers, somehow. If we continued to do business like this, The Bearded Goat would be out of business before I could run it.

All in all, the staff was efficient, nothing I couldn't work with. There were even a few who I would consider for management. They worked hard and I appreciated it.

But, this Penny Marks, now standing around twiddling her thumbs, doing nothing, tested my patience. I stood behind her as she polished a liquor bottle, and my anger heightened.

"Would you *please* clean?" I asked, stooping to her childish level.

She held up the bottle she was wiping, glancing at me through the large mirror behind the bar. "I am cleaning, Mr. Sullivan," she said in an overly exaggerated sarcastic voice. Irritation rose inside of me. She couldn't even take a second to turn around to face me.

"Cut the crap, Penny." I cracked my knuckles in annoyance as my eyes tightened. "You're polishing a bottle."

She spun around with wide eyes to face me. Her breathing picked up and her cheeks reddened with either embarrassment or anger—at this point I didn't care which.

"Excuse me, sir. The bottles get dirty when we pour drinks. If we don't polish the bottles then we'll get fruit flies. Do you want flies?"

"Of course I don't want flies." I leaned back against the bar. "Did you have a nice chat with Fiona?"

Her mouth hung open and the sassy expression was replaced with guilt. "Um, I can explain," she said.

"Save it, Penny. Let me explain something to you. Do your job, show up on time, and work hard and maybe in a year we can discuss the management thing again."

"A year? You're kidding right?"

I cracked a smile. "Sure, of course I am. I would never say a year. Maybe two."

"Oh ha ha very funny, Mr. Sullivan."

"You can call me Theo, as for the management position, try not to talk bad about me anymore."

"Theo, I didn't mean to be…"

"There's a lot you don't know about me. I never fail at anything I set my mind to. You best be remembering that."

"Oh I remember things quite vividly." Her eyes flashed to mine, and a hazy spark of recognition flickered and extinguished. I shook my head. I never saw her before; I was sure of it.

She was pretty the way her bangs fell right above her eyebrows. And this type of thought would have me out of business in a heartbeat. So, I would *not* be tempted.

I would keep her at arm's length and not let myself be attracted to her. She was an employee and not a very good one.

"Ok, get back to work," I said.

She shot me a look, and I grinned, leaning in close to her ear. "*Please.*" Big mistake, my cock pulsed. She brushed a hand across her cheek as she swiped away a strand of hair, and I wanted nothing more than to feel the softness of her skin. Her body trembled slightly and I stepped away.

"Yes sir," she breathed.

"Also, next time you decide to open your mouth," *That pretty little mouth,* "and trash talk me," *You'd blush at how filthy I talk,* "or call me an asshole..." *You'll get an ass spanking.* I faltered, unable to focus my thoughts as she stared at me curiously. What the fuck was happening? My dick throbbed. "Just remember, I'm your boss, and I'm not going anywhere. Decide if you can handle it."

She took in a deep breath as her expression hardened. "I won't quit," she said after a moment of silence.

"Fine." Grabbing a black server tray to hide my growing erection, I stalked away and left her there.

"Oh, and Theo," she called after me.

God, would she stop talking already? The last thing I needed her to see was the massive hard on I sported in my trousers.

I stopped dead in my tracks and glanced over my shoulder. "Yeah?"

"If you're interested, they have a ton of books on running a bar. It may come in handy." Her underhanded comment, disguised as helpful, grated on every nerve in my body and my jaw tensed.

I shook my head. "Get back to work," I retorted through clenched teeth.

She smiled wide. "Sure thing, boss."

I stormed out of the bar area and into the tiny office off of the kitchen.

I couldn't even talk to this girl for five minutes without my anger boiling over and my cock getting hard.

Who the hell did she think she was? Queen bartender? Give me a fucking break.

By evening, I made it home to my two-bedroom condo. The first week of owning a bar didn't go how I envisioned. My general manager quit, and I had a bartender who'd been given a glowing recommendation for management, but required a major attitude adjustment, which only turned me on more. All week long Penny continually shot me a perplexed stare every time I voiced an opinion or idea. There were two customers in the bar this afternoon, how difficult was it to stop and say goodbye as they left? Not fucking hard to me.

My phone pinged with an incoming call and I glanced at the caller ID. Fuck, Blair. What did she want?

I debated on ignoring the call, but after the third ring, I answered.

"What?" I huffed into the phone.

"Hello, Mr. Moody. What's got your panties in a bunch?"

"What do you want, Blair?" I rubbed a hand across my forehead. Her games were the last thing I wanted at the moment. Cracking open a beer and putting this mess of a day behind me were the only things appealing to me right now.

"You're still coming this weekend to grab Lucy, correct?"

"Why would you think I wouldn't be?" I asked, reaching in the fridge for a beer.

"I'm just checking."

"Then I'll be there. Haven't missed a time yet."

"Alright then," she huffed. "See you soon." She hung up without saying goodbye, and I didn't blame her. My attitude was borderline pure asshole and instead of taking my frustration out on the person who caused it, Penny Marks, Blair felt the brunt force of it.

I tossed my phone down on the black granite countertop and clasped my hands behind my head. What a fucking mess. It was now clear, the previous owner of the Bearded Goat fucking lied and I fell for it. Also, the pressing issue of my employees thinking I didn't know what I was doing created havoc on my system.

I put the beer back in the fridge, unopened, and made my way down the hallway. Inside the bathroom I grasped the marble sink with both hands and leaned over, staring into the mirror. A look of defeat stared back at me. Fuck that. I wasn't going to give up. Pushing off the counter, I removed my clothes.

I turned the shower on and stepped inside the glass stall, the hot water relaxed me instantly.

My cock grew heavy as I tugged it firm. I needed to come. I'd wanted to jerk off since the second I laid eyes on Penny at the bar. Her smile intoxicated me, and her eyes were like a well-worn penny casting her hatred at me. Her tight ass and tanned slender legs did things to me, wicked things. Things I should bury deep away in the bottom of my mind. Mostly though, it was the freckles, a splattering of a few light brown freckles which crossed over the bridge of her nose. I shouldn't jerk off to her—it was so fucking wrong.

Instead, I tried my damndest to conjure up my silver moon goddess from months prior.

"Fuck," I said on a groan, my balls heavy with lust. I tried to remember the way I slammed into her from behind and how she felt as I took her to new heights. Her pussy wet just for me.

How would Penny's wet pussy feel? *No, stop thinking about her, think about the goddess.*

I fixated back to the beach, the moon and stars shining down on us as I fucked the gorgeous woman who haunted my dreams at night.

I stroked along my cock remembering the way her skin tasted as I trailed my tongue along her neck. I pumped harder—fuck I wanted her again.

"Oh, God." My panting picked up as I braced a hand against the wall.

My mind played tricks on me as Penny's golden hair sprang through my consciousness and I clutched my cock tighter. Stroking my dick, which ached for one moment with her, down to my balls, I tried to push away the thoughts of Penny. *Get out of my head.*

I grunted, loudly. The sound echoed off the tile. I groaned not able to fight my mind any longer against her.

The hot water cascaded over me as images of Penny in her bright pink tank crashed through my mind.

Pressing my hand harder on the shower tiles my cock throbbed.

Closing my eyes, fantasies of Penny naked, slowly exhaling and panting from arousal were taking over. I'd take a handful of her hair slick from the wetness of the water, wanting control, and kneel her before me. Her shining eyes would gaze up to mine—captivating and hungry. God, she'd be perfect below me, taking my cock in her sweet, open mouth.

"Damn," I moaned.

My arm flexed as I tightened my hold. Pumping, throbbing, and needing her more than I wanted to admit.

I squeezed my eyes shut, fucking my hand, and enjoying every moment of it.

I grunted as I picked up speed. Her head bobbing in between my legs played in my mind like a slideshow.

My arm grew weak trying to hold myself up, the hot water scalding my skin, my hand pumping vigorously as I imagined Penny's sweet lips sucking me off.

What would she feel like? I was so close to coming I couldn't stop the rapid images flashing behind my closed lids. Big, round tits. Sucking them in my mouth. Biting her nipples. She was so fucking hot.

As I grew closer, my thoughts shifted as I imagined slamming her against the tile and fucking her hot, wet cunt.

My breathing was heavy and my body was in agony from not having her here, her tight pussy wrapped around me, her body begging for my touch. The muscles in my thighs tightened as soon as I felt the first wave of my orgasm rip through me. Fuck, I wanted her.

I jerked my hand faster as I came hard, my chest heaving from the force of it.

Damn. I wanted her the hell out of my bar and my head.

I needed to make a list. Lists always made me feel better. I toweled off and slipped on a pair of black gym shorts.

Not bothering with a shirt, I made my way into my bedroom. After grabbing a pen and spiral notebook from the drawer of the nightstand, I settled into bed and flipped on my Boondock Saints night lamp and started writing.

REASONS TO FIRE PENNY
- Her attitude
- Her complete lack of respect for authority
- Her sassiness
- ~~The guests really do like her~~

I paused briefly before furiously crossing through the line when I thought about the way they did in fact like her. Can't fire her for that. Shaking my head, tapping my pen on the notebook, I narrowed my eyes. Back to the list.

- Her complete lack of regard for me
    - ~~The way she smiles at me~~

Ok, this list wasn't working out well. I wasn't finding any real reasons. I thought long and hard for anything which would warrant firing her.

- Late

Chewing on the top of my pen, I stared at the word *Late* scribbled on the paper. It really was a one-time thing, and she'd been on time since then. Actually, she was usually early. It remained on the list anyways. Maybe I should make a list about what to do to get rid of her. I crumbled the paper and tossed it to the floor.

New List How to get rid of Penny

- Fire her

No, I guess I couldn't outright fire her. It would probably cause more problems for me. Think.

- Ride her harder at work, so maybe she'll quit

Yeah, I'd ride her ass hard. Ok, thoughts like these weren't helping. They got me in this mess. What could I do to get rid of her? Maybe a list of what to do to stop thinking about her would help.

New New List How to Stop Thinking About Penny

- Make her wear a long sleeve shirt.
  - No makeup at work
    - Freckleectomy

Did they have a surgery to remove freckles? I could always add it to the list to find out. Either way Operation Forget Freckles was now underway.

- Focus on anything else

What could I do to stop thinking about her? She was slowly creeping in. I clutched the pen tighter in my hand as I freed my mind and started writing.

- Read more
- Search high and low for the Boba Fett action figure (priority)
- Watch Star Wars over and over until you have every line memorized

- Buy a new video game (GTA is coming out)
- Play the video game until my fingers break
- Stop staring at her
- Tell her she's no longer allowed to talk at work

Fuck, this list was pointless. I yanked the paper from the spiral notebook and crushed it into my fists. Throwing it into the air, I cursed again.

I rubbed my eyes as I threw the notebook and pen across the room.

Flicking off the lamp, I tossed a while until sleep finally pulled me under.

When I entered the bar, bright and early, I found Penny behind the bar, leaning over into the beer cooler with her ass in the air. Rooted to the spot, my eyes lingered longer than they should have.

Her heart-shaped ass begged to be smacked by my flat palm. Yes, exactly what she needed, a good ass spanking. Unable to look away, I watched as she stretched her tight body upright before she turned and saw me gaping at her.

"Oh, Theo. I didn't see you there."

"Right," I clipped. "How could you with your ass in my face?"

She took in a sharp gasp of air before a scarlet stain spread across her chest.

"Why don't you bend at the knees from now on, Penny." Fuck. A vision of her kneeling in front of me raced through my mind.

Her pouty lips pressed into a thin line before she turned, setting the Samuel Adams bottles on the glossy, oak bar. "Maybe you should post a sign," she muttered.

"And where should I post this sign? On your ass that's always in my face?"

"Well, you'd be the only one reading it since you seem to always be staring at it."

"Me, stare at your ass? No, not likely. It's common knowledge you bend from the knees to pick something up."

"Like this?" She lowered to the ground, bending her knees in a sexy squat before me and I couldn't think straight as she slowly rose up from it.

We were standing inches apart, and my body buzzed with excitement. "I'm sure that's not what they intended when they made that rule."

She propped a hip against the wash sink and crossed her arms. "No? And just what did they intend?"

"To not stick your ass in people's faces, I presume."

"Yeah, we wouldn't want that." Her eyes grew wide in mock horror. "Call the back police, there's an ass in my face. Hey, look officer, there's an ass right there," she said, pointing directly at me.

I leaned in closer. "You think you're so fucking smart, don't you?"

"Maybe a little."

"We'll see how smart you are when your back's broken."

She laughed and the sound was like nails on a chalkboard. A really fucking sexy chalkboard. "Thanks, Theo, for always watching out for my backside."

"Ok, enough sass from you. Let's get to work."

"Sure thing, boss." She saluted me.

A fucking salute. My frustration with her grew as she smiled sweetly which was in complete contrast to her sour attitude.

"Today you'll be showing me exactly what it is you do here."

My plan was to watch her closely and find a reason to get rid of her.

After an hour of her showing me all the liquors and how to pour a beer from the tap, I realized there was more to bartending than I previously believed.

A group of women entered the bar and seated themselves right before me. Confidence coursed through my veins. I felt more in my element. Maybe I didn't know how to pour a drink, but I sure knew how to take care of the ladies. I made my way over to the group of twenty-something year olds dressed in their beach wear and leaned an arm against the bar.

"Can I help you ladies?" I gave them a lazy grin and they giggled. There were five women in all, and each one ordered a Cosmopolitan.

"Penny, five Cosmos," I called over my shoulder.

A moment later, Penny slammed a shaker, a bottle of vodka, triple sec, and some cranberry juice in front of me.

"Here you go. Have fun." She gave me a slight smile, which didn't reach her eyes, and stalked off to the opposite end of the bar

Fuck. I can fake this shit.

I scooped some ice into the stainless steel shaker and poured the vodka in first. I poured for a while then, added the triple sec and cranberry juice. Easy. I topped the shaker and shook like I'd seen in the movies.

Grabbing a few martini glasses, the ones I always saw women in the clubs drink their cosmos from, I lined them on the bar and poured away. Two drinks down. I repeated the process until all five glasses were filled.

Owned that shit.

The ladies laughed as I slid over their drinks, winking to each one.

The brunette took a sip and turned her nose up as she tried to swallow it down.

"Is this a Cosmo?" she asked as she set the drink along the bar.

The other girls all took a sip with the same reaction as I tugged at the back of my neck with my hand. "What's wrong, ladies?"

"Sorry, it doesn't taste right."

I examined the drinks and they were fucking pink. What did I do wrong? "Penny," I said over my shoulder. "Can you come make the Cosmos for these lovely women?"

I emptied the five drinks into the sink as Penny stomped over.

"Fine, *Boss*," she said through clamped teeth and a fake smile. She made the drinks like a pro, all while trying to show me the process.

When the new drinks were finished, I slid them over to the group of chicks.

"Thank you. What's your name? Are you new here?" one of the girls asked.

"Yep, and you can come back to see me anytime." I glanced at Penny as I said the next line. "Because I'm not going anywhere."

After telling them all my name, I joked and laughed with them, trying my best to keep them entertained while I left Penny to handle the rest of the bar.

For a Tuesday afternoon we weren't slammed, but Penny appeared busy as she shot me her evil glare every so often. I laughed to myself—yeah suck it up.

SIX

PENNY

I was livid. Lord of The Assholes is what he was.

Here I thought maybe Theo took this whole learning the ropes thing seriously, but no, he wanted an excuse to flirt with the locals.

The ladies at the bar who hung on his every word were annoying me to no end. I couldn't even glance in his direction.

Calm down. Why are you so mad?

I ran my hand across the bar and thought about Dex. It'd been another day of radio silence and worry about his whereabouts started to creep in. Why didn't he call?

Everyone and everything annoyed me today. Rage lurked below the surface of my smile, threatening to surge out, but I knew I should keep it together through this shift.

Once I got home, I would blow Dex's phone up until he answered. Or maybe I'd take a nap and forget about them both: Dex and Theo.

A Jason Mraz song played in the bar as everyone clapped and laughed along. I looked out at the guests we had this afternoon, so happy, carefree, and loving life. The complete opposite of me. Against my better judgement, I snuck a glance over at Theo. He was gorgeous with his dark, piercing eyes and chiseled jaw. His forearms rested on the bar and he was transfixed by something a redhead said to him. As she spoke, her arm waved wildly in the air, her fruity drink sloshing out, and he threw his head back and laughed.

I guess I was lucky he didn't remember me. He probably picked up women every night, and I wasn't any different to the many faceless one-nighters he had previously. It pissed me off thinking about how shallow he was. I didn't normally do those things—one night stands weren't *my* thing.

I wished I could turn off the sector of my brain that found him sexy and made me want to touch him in places the sun didn't shine. I could never go there again, not if I wanted to keep my job. I shook my head and grabbed a towel to wipe down the bar. I didn't want to give him any more reasons to find fault with me. Ugh.

Why did I have to go and stick my foot in my big mouth?

I decided right then and there, I would not let the past dictate my future. So what, I called him a few names. Get over it.

While he flirted with the five bimbos, I'd make myself useful and run this whole bar alone, and do an excellent job. I would prove myself worthy of this job and the promotion I deserved. Theo would see I could run this bar and be an asset doing so.

I threw the towel under the counter and grabbed a few tickets as they shot out of the printer. One more glance from me slid his way before I made the drinks for the cocktail waitresses.

Glancing up, I noticed Margo bouncing her way to the bar, and a huge smile spread across my lips. She pushed past people to make her way over, wearing a red sundress with her bikini straps peeking out from the top.

"Hey, Penny," she said, leaning over the bar to kiss my cheek. "I had to come in and see you..." She stopped and I followed her line of vision directly to Theo.

"Hey," I said, trying to get her attention. I waved a hand in front of her face as she leaned back trying to catch a better glimpse of the new boss.

"Is that him?" she whispered. "Mr. Hoity-Toity?"

"Yeah, he's the new owner."

Her face turned to mine and her eyes were wide with disbelief. "Really?"

"Yes."

"Are you kidding? He's hot. You're so lucky."

I rolled my eyes.

"Sure," I huffed as I turned to pour her usual drink of Malibu Rum and pineapple.

She stared a bit longer at Theo and then returned her attention back to me as she slid her shapely body onto a bar stool. I passed her drink to her and she took a sip before speaking. "I came to see you to tell you a story. Remember the guy I told you about?"

"The one from your gym?" I snuck a quick glance over to Theo who was still engrossed in a conversation with one of the floozies.

"Yes, the fighter. Well, today when I left the gym he said goodbye." She beamed as she stirred the black straw in her yellow drink.

I smiled at her, indulgently. "What are you in seventh grade? Maybe you can pass him a note during third period," I teased.

"Shut up. This is a big deal." She giggled. "You know I've been trying to get his attention for weeks."

She tried many different things to gain the awareness of a certain MMA fighter who worked out at the same gym she did. Ripped with muscles in places I didn't know muscles existed, he never gave poor Margo the time of day—well until today.

"You're right. It *is* a big deal. What did you say?"

She twisted on the stool trying desperately to contain her excitement. "I said goodbye back."

I shook my head and laughed. "Oh god, Margo. You rushed down here to tell me this?"

"Of course not. I rushed down here to get a drink and soak up the sun. It's my day off, but I also wanted to tell you about sexy fighter guy."

We didn't have a name for the unknown muscled man, but we were currently working on the small detail. And by working on it, Margo asked everyone at the gym for the mystery man's name.

As I laughed I felt body heat radiate behind me, and then Theo's koi fish tattooed arm reached around me as he extended it out to Margo for a handshake. "And who is this lovely lady here?" he asked with a hint of playfulness in his voice.

"This lovely lady is Margo, Penny's roommate and best friend," Margo said, extending her hand out. "You're the boss, huh?"

They shook hands and my body stiffened as his chest pressed against my back. I side-stepped out of his way so they could continue the conversation I no longer cared to hear.

Theo was 'the boss' and he sure liked everyone to know it. I moved over to a lone man standing at the bar and offered him a drink.

"I'll take a blow job," the blond-haired man said, winking.

"One blow job shot, coming up." As I turned away, he reached across the bar and grabbed my arm.

He leered at me. "No, I'll just take a blow job."

I lowered my glare to where he still held my elbow, his stubby fingers digging into my skin, and tried to yank my arm away.

"Let go of me, *now*," I said through clenched, tight lips.

His beady eyes swept over my body. "You're a pretty little thing."

66

"And you're about to be a dead little thing," Theo's forceful voice sounded from behind me. "Let go of the lady and let me walk you to the door."

"I'm not done talking to her yet," blond guy said.

"The fuck you are," Theo said.

"Who the hell do you think you are?" blond guy questioned.

Theo, in one fell swoop, leapt across the bar. It was sexy as hell. He slammed the man's face down and leaned down to his ear. "I'm the owner, and I'm throwing you the fuck out." Still gripping the man by the back of his neck, Theo led him to the door.

Margo rushed over to where I stood.

"Did that really happen?" She took a seat, all of her attention focused on Theo and the raucous ensuing.

Theo was in a heated discussion with the blond guy, and by the time Seth made his way over to offer back up, Theo had the jerk out of the door.

"Yeah, that guy's an asshole." I rubbed my elbow, my eyes glued to the action at the entrance as well.

"He's like some hot as hell superhero," she said, turning to me.

"It's him," I leaned in and whispered, "The Lord of my O's."

Her brows shot up. "Are you serious?" She looked over at Theo and then back to me. "Penny, what are the chances of The Lord of your O's buying this bar?"

I lifted my brows at her. "Apparently excellent."

After kicking the guy out, Theo rushed over, taking my elbow in his hands, glancing it over. "Are you ok?" he asked.

"Yeah, I'm used to it." I shrugged.

He locked eyes with me. "No one will touch you again while I'm around. I won't have anyone manhandling *my* employees."

"Thanks for helping, but I can take care of myself, just so you know." I held his stare as he dropped my arm.

"It's my job to protect my workers."

His sincerity caught me off guard and a current of want flowed through my body, settling in my core.

"Thanks," I muttered as he walked away.

"Oh, damn. I can't believe he's the guy from the beach. It must be fate," Margo said in an all too self-assured voice. She walked back over to her previous spot at the bar and grabbed her drink. "I'll be over on a lounger wishing I was you."

"He doesn't even remember who I am," I whispered to myself as she walked away.

A few days later, Dex called before I left for work. When I mentioned Theo Sullivan he sat silent for a moment and then told me to stay away from him. When I questioned why, he abruptly cut the conversation short. This behavior was odd and out of character for Dex. When we first met he was so charming, and lately he'd turned into something different.

Chaos greeted me when I walked into work. It was a later shift, and the afternoon rush destroyed the bar. The liquor order wasn't put away, and I didn't see anyone manning the bar.

I let out a sigh and threw my handbag into its usual spot. "Who worked today?" I asked Fiona. "This place is a disaster."

"Theo worked the bar himself to cut labor costs."

"And now he'll pay someone else to clean up after him." I threw my hair into a messy bun and glanced at the floors covered in trash. Theo stepped around the corner of the bar and our eyes met.

"Hey, Penny, the liquor order needs to be put away," he called out to me. "Can you get to it?" He brushed past me with a case of Amstel Light in his hands and set it down along the bar to refill the cooler. "Also, the bar could use a little cleaning before the dinner rush."

I rolled my eyes to Fiona as she laughed. "Normally, the person working the day shift takes care of the liquor order," I said as he removed bottles. "You would know this, if you knew anything about a bar." Frustrated with how he always left the bar in complete disarray, I huffed out an agitated breath.

His arm stilled and he turned his head slowly my way. A muscle ticked in his jaw. Hard flints in his eyes followed my movement as I slowly bent down into a squat and flourished my arm to grab the receiving order clipboard from the lower shelf. "Wouldn't want to hurt my back." I smiled and stalked off toward the kitchen to take care of the order after he rolled his eyes.

As I put away a few bottles of Tanqueray in the liquor cabinet, I realized Theo would never take me seriously.

I'd never be moved from a lowly worker into a position of power. Maybe my father was right. Maybe bartending was a dead end job.

But, right now it was a means to an end. A stepping stone to a bigger dream.

I worked diligently to put away the cases of liquor. As each bottle hit the shelves, my hatred built like a full force hurricane.

When I finally finished, I ventured behind the bar to find every liquor bottle in the wrong place. Dirty bar glasses lined the wash sink, and it appeared as if Theo didn't clean a thing.

"This bar is trashed," I said, glancing at the fruit tray with no freshly cut fruit for the cocktails.

"Yeah." Bottles clinked as he filled the cooler.

"Why didn't you cut any fruit for the night shift?" He leaned up, finally giving me his attention, and I pointed to the tray as he ran a hand through his hair.

"Can't you do it?"

I didn't like his tone and I grew frustrated with his lack of teamwork. "I guess I'll have to," I said, snatching up the empty tray. "Usually the bartender for the day shift does it though."

"Well, I'm not a bartender, I'm the boss."

"Yes, I've noticed you're not a very good bartender. Fiona," I called out, "could you get me a pen and paper? We may need another sign. Theo here is the boss." The words slid out before I could stop them.

I moved to go past him and he reached out an arm blocking me. "Are you kidding? I'm not here to do your busy work, Penny." He leveled me with a patronizing stare. "That's what I pay you for."

My face turned hot as I thought about what he said. Busy work? My workload had doubled because of him and I fought down my anger not to blow up. I wanted to mouth off more to him but didn't want to risk pushing him too far.

I went to the kitchen and slammed down the tray. Grabbing a cutting board and knife, I got to work, chopping out my frustration. While slaving away, I sliced into the tip of my middle finger and dropped the knife.

This was all Theo's fault. Lord of the Signs.

I ran my finger under the faucet and again my thoughts flew to Theo and his forehead I wanted so badly to flick.

After bandaging myself up and finishing off the fruit, I returned to the bar. Theo waited with his arms crossed over his chest.

"What took you so long? I need to get out of here for the night."

"Sorry, I cut my finger." I stuck my middle bandaged finger up to him in a fuck you type of way.

"Practice makes perfect. Maybe you should be the only person to cut all the fruit from now on."

"You can't make me do that."

He stalked closer as I lowered my finger. "I can make you do whatever I want. You want to know why?"

"Yeah, because you're the boss. I get it. But, you should learn you can't treat your employees this way. Pretty soon, you'll have none left."

He laughed. "Bartenders are a dime a dozen. I'll always be able to find someone hungry for a job."

"Good luck," I said, biting my tongue as he walked away.

Once again I was left to clean up the disaster which was Theo Sullivan.

SEVEN

THEO

What a shitty week. This bar would break me if Penny didn't first.

After sitting in my office at the Bearded Goat, I decided I would need to seriously figure something out to keep this bar afloat. The past two weeks were a testament to how bad off this bar truly was. The only good things about my days were getting a rise out of Penny.

I took great pleasure in seeing the crimson flush of anger creep up her neck when I made her clean the seagull shit off the back patio after she poured my drink into a baby bottle.

I then went and took the Roses Lime Juice and poured it over the liquor bottles and watched as the bottles slipped from her hands while she tried to serve the guests. It was unprofessional but I didn't give a shit. The next day she'd sent me a "Running a Bar For Dummies" book. She'd left it on my desk with a note telling me to read up.

One instance, of Penny engrossed in a book, kept replaying over in my mind. It was a rainy day and the bar was empty. She was zoned out, bent over the bar, her chin resting in her palm. I walked up behind her and cleared my throat.

She jumped. "Shit, you scared me."

"Are you reading about how to bartend?" I grabbed the book from her hands and flipped it open, reading aloud,

"She lay with her legs spread wide before him as he stared longingly at her. Her heart beat faster as he closed the space between them.
With a wild passion burning through his system, he struck out his tongue to taste the sweet nectar she possessed."

"Give it back," she demanded, reaching for the book.

"What is this smut?" I turned away from her and continued reading,

"His throbbing member entered her love slit as she moaned loudly. "Make me come, Thorne."
His jagged movements brought Babette to her own tumultuous orgasm."

"It's not smut, it's romance." Her tits pressed against my back as she tried to reach for the book I held in the air.

"No this is smut. What the hell is a love slit? Do you enjoy reading these filthy books?" It felt personal to be knowing these intimate details but, what the fuck was she reading this stuff for at *my* bar?

"Yes, I love these books. Now give it back." Her temper rose as she once again reached for the book.

"Oh right, here's your book," I said, handing it to her, trying not to think about her reading alone at home, late at night. "I guess you need to get some ideas."

"Maybe *you* should." She leaned down, stuffing the book in her handbag under the bar. "You wouldn't know the first thing about romance."

"Romance? What do I need to read a smutty book about romance for? I do just fine."

"It's better than the comic books I've seen piled in your office."

I took a deep breath, my smile faltering. "They're graphic novels, there's a difference." I crossed my arms. "Besides, at least my books don't talk about pulverizing a pussy to smithereens."

Her cheeks turned a bright crimson as she propped a hip against the bar.

"Well maybe you're not mature enough to read about pussies since you're obsessed with those cartoon books."

I cocked a brow. "Cartoon books? Again, they're graphic novels. And you're right, I don't need to read about pussy. I can always go out and get it."

"Yeah, I'm sure you're The Lord of One-Nighters." Her bangs blew off her forehead as she made a pfft sound.

"Is that an offer?"

"No. Never." She was angry. I could tell by the way her face scrunched up, and I noticed the freckles along the bridge of her nose. She really was quite adorable, but I wouldn't allow a second glance her way.

Every fucking day it was something with her. But, I realized she knew her shit and the regulars adored her. At first I ignored her, I pretended she didn't exist. Yet, working in the tight confines of the bar, and having her tits brush up against me occasionally during the rush, it became harder to not think about her—really fucking hard. I pushed away thoughts of her everyday but at night the thoughts came back with a vengeance and pushed me over the edge to the depths of hell.

She teased me daily with the way she bent over to get things and her ass would press against me. Or the way the Bearded Goat tank barely held her breasts in and her nipples would harden after a visit to the cooler. Sometimes her bangs would hang in her eyes and I would have to fight the urge to brush them off her face. It became too much to bear. I needed to get my shit together and figure things out with this bar so I didn't have to be here everyday. Especially with the summer months around the corner. Most high-society wintered in Florida, creating enough business to usually keep many businesses up and running through the summer. Not the Bearded Goat.

I slammed the quarterly reports down on my desk and ran a hand across my face. *Fuck.*

My mind wandered briefly to my silver moon goddess and our one fateful night many months ago. Where was she?

Thinking of her, and the way she disappeared made me angry. I pushed away from the desk and decided a drink was in order. I would head over to the neighboring clubs and see what trouble I could get into for the evening.

We didn't normally have a big night crowd, so leaving Seth to handle the place was a no brainer. Turning out the lights, I left the bar. As I walked down Ocean Drive, Mekka shook with energy and adrenaline. I opened the glass door and nodded to the bouncer who stood guard as I walked inside.

The dance floor was packed with sweaty bodies as they rocked to the loud beat of the bass.

Neon lights and glass tables were all the eye could see. A bit of overstimulation but they were packed, so they must have been doing something right.

"Macallan neat," I called to the man behind the fiberglass bar.

He poured the brown-stained liquor straight from the bottle and slid the drink my way. I threw a few bills down as I took a swig of the whiskey.

The pounding of the music vibrated through my body as I watched a few scantily dressed ladies float by. The further I ventured into the club the more I wished away all the anxiety I felt the past few weeks.

I scanned the club once more and my eyes landed on a lightly-freckled nose. It scrunched at me when our eyes met.

It took me a moment to actually recognize her, wait, yes it *was* her and what the fuck was she wearing? Christ, she looked like a slut and my mouth watered at the sight of her.

Her heels rocked back and forth as she swayed to the music without a care in the world.

The way she eye fucked me was sexy, and I couldn't stand here and take it any longer. She teased me, like she did every damn day at the bar. Filled with irritation, I stalked over.

She danced next to her blonde friend whose name was not coming to mind. Nothing came to mind. Only a dirty reel of images of Penny taking off everything she wore except the black high heeled-shoes with the tiny pink bows on her feet. They were sweet, too sweet, and the sight of them made my cock pulse.

She didn't acknowledge me until I practically stood right next to her.

"Oh, it's you," she slurred as she placed a hand on her friend's shoulder to steady herself. "Don't bother me. I'm trying to have fun, something you know nothing about."

"I know how to have fun. But you're right, I only came over here to chat with your friend." I took her friend's hand in mine and laid a kiss on her yellow polished nails. *Margo? Marlo?*

"Hi there, again," her friend giggled.

"Margo." Penny slapped her friend's hand from mine, and I smiled at the jealous expression on her beautiful face.

"What's wrong, Penny? Don't want me having fun with your friend here?"

"There are a million women in here. Take your pick of any of them, and leave *us* alone." Her feet were unsteady as she waved a hand in my face.

With a quick snap, I gripped her wrist and yanked her body closer. "Let's get one thing straight. I'm the boss, stop telling me what to do," I hissed never breaking eye contact.

"Ok, on that note, I'll see you two later. Penny, I'll be right over there at the bar if you need me," Margo said as she left Penny and me standing toe to toe with my hold on her tightening.

"How dare you speak to me that way," Penny said with a fiery passion in her voice.

It turned me on—fucking fierce.

She taunted me, made me feel stupid for not knowing as much as she did, and I wanted to let her know I wouldn't stand for it any longer.

"How dare I? Do you know who you're talking to?"

"Yeah, my jerkface boss." Her words fanned across my lips, and I could taste the liquor on her breath.

Her pulse quickened, and it throbbed under my fingertips. Without thinking, I turned around and kept a hold of her as I led her through the dance club. A dark hallway to the restroom was lit by one tiny pink neon light and I slammed her against the wall. "You want me to kiss you, don't you?" I asked, gripping her waist with both hands. I pressed my cock into the spot between her legs so she could feel how hard I was for her.

Her arms flew around my neck as she clung to me tighter. She rocked her hips and I knew this affected her as much as me.

Her eyes were heavy with desire as I brushed my hand along her shoulder, finally feeling her soft silky skin. "This little black dress is fucking slutty. Why would you wear this? Do you like to tease, Penny?"

Her mouth opened and I could see the rage on her face. She took a deep breath and before she could speak I raised my finger, pressing her lips closed and shook my head back and forth. "You stay quiet, and stop teasing me."

She sucked my finger into her mouth and my eyes fell closed. Fuck, it felt surreal until I felt her teeth clamp down around my skin, drawing blood.

"What the fuck, Penny." I pulled my finger from her bite, examining it.

"I'm not teasing you. I hate you," she spewed her venom and my heart raced harder.

"You're a fucking tease. You don't see the way you're flaunting your tight little body for every man to see tonight?" I pulled her harder against me as my throbbing cock needed attention. "Do you want to see how it feels to be teased, Penny?" *Oh, I'll give her a taste of her own medicine.*

"Are you kidding me? Every woman here tonight is dressed like me, some even worse."

"I won't allow you to dress like a little tramp and turn me on. Jesus, your tits are spilling out of the top of your dress," I said with my lips inches from hers.

"Allow?"

I backed away slightly as I gazed at her dress one more time and licked my full hungry lips. Teasing her as bad as she teased me these past few weeks was the only thing on my mind.

"Yes. You look so fuckable right now, Penny, and I don't like it."

"Fuck you, asshole," she said as her fingers tightened on my neck, her nails digging deep as she pulled me closer.

"Fuck me? No, fuck you." I ran my nose along her soft skin, breathing in the tasty smell of her body.

What was I doing? This was insanity.

"Oh God, Theo."

My name tripped from her lips and I angled closer to whisper in her ear. "Are you wet, Penny? I bet if I ran my fingers along your pussy, you'd be soaked." She gasped at my words. "Would you like it if I pressed on your clit and pumped my fingers so deep in-fucking-side you? I bet you've never come as hard as I can make you."

"No," she said as she rocked her hips against me, grazing her teeth along her bottom lip.

"I bet if I finger fucked you, your pussy's so tight. So sweet, dripping down my hand." Her head fell back against the wall and she let out a breathy moan. A low growl rumbled from me feeling her sweet cunt grind against my dick. *Oh God, I was so fucking hard.*

"And then after you come on my hand, I'd smear it all over your tits and suck it off. You want me to, don't you? Tell me how bad you want me to suck your wet nipples into my mouth and bite down, making you scream my name," I demanded, my heart racing.

"Please, stop," she begged, rocking herself against me. Her words said one thing, but the hunger in her eyes told me she wanted this as badly as I did.

"Penny, you fucking tease me. I bet you smell so good and I bet you taste even better." Drunk from the want pouring through my veins, I needed to bury my thick cock in her, balls deep.

"Do you want your little pussy to come all over me? My fingers. My face. My fucking cock." I braced both hands against the wall beside her, boxing her in. My lips brushed hers lightly as I spoke, "Do you like it when I tease you, Penny?"

"Oh God yes, I mean no," she whimpered, her fingers twisting through my hair.

"You need to stop. I can't handle it," I whispered. She needed to learn she couldn't tease me anymore.

"I'm sorry," she murmured.

She groaned as her body arched into me. It was too intense, my senses overloaded as I made the mistake of gazing at her face. Her eyes squeezed shut, her cheeks flushed from arousal, and the god damn freckles along the bridge of her nose were too much. I stepped back and her eyes flew open. Her chest rose and fell as she stared back at me. *What the fuck happened?*

I lowered my forehead to rest along hers, whispering, "Penny, I've never been a good guy, and I can't handle what you do to me."

"I have a boyfriend," she cut me off.

My heart beat through my disbelieving ears. Disappointment washed over me, drowning me. I couldn't believe the words she spoke which stabbed me with their jagged meaning.

"Fuck." I squeezed my eyes shut, punching my fist at the wall.

Shaking my head, I walked away from her, beelining straight for the exit.

Run, was the only thing on my mind as I raced to my car.

Run from this girl and her beautiful eyes and her cute fucking freckles.

Once seated inside I took a heavy breath.

I slammed my hand on the steering wheel.

Fuck, I wasn't expecting any of that.

I needed to eighty-six Penny once and for all.

I almost went too far, I was ready to take her right then and there, fuck her up against the wall in Mekka, a few nights before, until she mentioned a boyfriend and shell-shocked my entire system. Which lucky for me she stopped things, because wanting her should be the furthest thing from my mind.

Now, Operation Get Rid of Penny's Ass was my only mission.

By the time Friday rolled around, I called Blair to tell her I was on my way over. She lived not too far from South Beach in a quiet neighborhood.

I climbed the brick steps leading up to her front porch and stopped, steeling myself, before I could knock. Blair was a touchy subject for me, and the thought of seeing her never got any easier. She'd been beautiful to me a lifetime ago, but now when I looked at her I only saw lies and deceit. After knocking on the bright red door, I thrust both hands into the pockets of my jeans and rocked on my heels as I waited.

"Hey, right on time," Blair said with her smile lighting up her hazel irises. Her long black hair was swept up into a bun, and she glanced over her shoulder as our daughter came running down the hallway behind her.

"Daddy, Daddy," Lucy called. Her brown-haired pigtails bounced with every step. Pushing past her mother, she leapt into my arms. Blair leaned against the doorway watching as I hugged her tight.

"Hey, Boo Bear," I said, calling her the nickname I created the moment she was born.

At three years old she held my heart in her tiny innocent hands.

Blair and I dated a few years back, and when she found out she was pregnant I wanted to marry her. I loved her, or so I thought.

On the day I planned to propose, I found her in our apartment fucking my half-brother and my heart shattered into a million pieces.

The worst part of the whole fiasco was the fact my daughter was inside her as she fucked him.

I blew up and never spoke to my brother again. Blair, however, was a different story. We shared joint custody of our daughter and I remained pleasant whenever I saw her, for Lucy's sake. Even though Blair tried desperately to creep back into my good graces ever since I left her, I would never forgive her betrayal.

"She just ate, so she's ready to go," Blair said, handing me Lucy's red backpack.

"Have fun, see you on Tuesday."

We waved goodbye, and I kissed Lucy's bright red cheeks as I carried her to the car.

"Ready to get out of here?" I asked as I buckled her into the car seat

"Ready," she squealed.

We were off and I couldn't wait to get her home. I missed her when she wasn't around.

Being a father changed my life, and my daughter was everything to me. Somedays, I didn't know how I would make it from one day to the next. Was I scared? Fuck yeah, I was. I worried about everything. Life was good as a real estate investor, and the bills were always paid. But the dream of one day owning a bar wasn't going away, and I wanted to give it a go. Living in South Beach the clubs along Ocean Drive were the pulse of the city. I wanted a piece of it.

And now at thirty years old, I sank most of my money into the Goat, and I needed this to work.

Life was hard though, finding love and companionship was a no-go.

Chaos, headaches, and utter madness were a part of my regular routine and I wouldn't have it any other way. The life of a single father left me little time for love.

EIGHT

PENNY

"I bet no one could make you come as hard as I can."
"You did," my mind screamed.

For the next two days after the club incident I never left my apartment. I cleaned, and cleaned some more. Sweeping, mopping, and scrubbing every part of the tile floors—anything to keep my mind occupied. Anything to not think about the look on Theo's face when I told him about my boyfriend. When he slammed his hand against the wall I felt the devastation pour off him.

I avoided Dex's phone calls. He called a few times over the past few weeks, and every time I asked about coming home he would have to rush off the phone. Confusion over everything took up residence deep within me. As much as I tried to think about anything else, Theo's hurt expression kept rolling through my overactive mind. I was a bitch for not stopping it sooner.

Having his hands on me was something I never thought I'd experience again. Or want, to be honest, after the way he treated me at the bar. My body pulled to his, fucking traitor, and I needed to stay far away.

I was the worst girlfriend ever.

When Saturday morning arrived, work was on the agenda.

As I finished getting ready, smoothing lotion down my legs, Margo threw herself on my bed.

"Fuck my life," she complained as she covered both arms over her eyes. Her blonde curly waves splayed over the bright orange pillowcase.

"What's wrong?" I asked, looking over at her.

She propped up onto her elbows and glared. "Hottie fighter has a whore girlfriend."

I sat down on the bed and wrapped an arm around her shoulder. "I'm sorry, Mar."

"It's ok. I'll figure it out or find someone new to stalk."

"Yeah," I whispered, barely listening.

"What's wrong? What happened with Theo at the club the other night?" She sat and waited for my answer.

"Nothing happened. Nothing at all." Part truth. He didn't touch me, but I felt the ghost of his hands everywhere.

I hated myself, completely hated myself. I hated how turned on I was. It was wrong. Dex should have been on my mind, but I couldn't focus with Theo's hot breath saying those things to me.

His filthy mouth I loved on the beach, now dripped with poison.

Once I arrived at work my stomach filled with butterflies. Dread set in at seeing Theo. Saturdays were busy, and I couldn't wait to drown all my nervous energy with tending to the happy guests who would need some liquor to enjoy their day further.

"Ready for a hot day?" Seth asked as I set up the bar.

"I heard it's going to be a scorcher." I threw my hair into a low ponytail.

"Yeah."

"Wish we had some fans." I felt the heat of the pending afternoon looming in the air.

The crowd picked up as we sweated to the sounds of Jimmy Buffett's 'Cheeseburger in Paradise' over and over.

What was it with Jimmy Buffett being the epitome of tiki bar music?

I worked the outside bar while Seth took care of the guests inside. Around three o'clock I went on my lunch break.

I decided to stroll the beach while I let the salty air flow across my skin. I stopped at a few of the vendor booths lined along the large sidewalk on Ocean Drive. Glancing at the jewelry for sale, I saw a beautiful turquoise bracelet with little turtle charms. The silver and blue sparkled in the sunlight. After purchasing the bracelet and slipping it onto my wrist, a squeal of laughter caught my attention.

Down by the water, I saw Theo chasing a small brown haired child in a pink swimsuit and knew instantly he wasn't lying the night we first met. I moved away from the jewelry booth and tried to get a closer look. He laughed as he grabbed her and lifted her above his shoulders.

What really made my jaw drop was the sight of him without a shirt. His shoulders were broad and his muscles lean. His sun-soaked body was lickable, and I remembered the one fateful night we shared when his body pumped inside me. A shiver skated across my arms and down my back.

After kicking off my tennis shoes and socks, I took a few steps onto the sandy beach. Theo and his daughter sat plopped down in the sand close to the shore, the waves crashing beyond them. He picked up a yellow shovel as she picked up a purple one and together they dug into the sand. I laughed quietly to myself as she tossed a shovel-full of sand in his lap and squealed with little girl giggles. Watching the carefree way he played with her made me doubt him to be the asshole I pegged him for.

I stalked closer as I watched. He lurched forward, picked her up, and tickled her.

I could hear her this time as she squawked and laughed calling out "Daddy" which in turn rooted me to the spot, I was too close.

It was sweet the way they played together and I smiled as I noticed the carefree expression on his gorgeous face. Without knowing it, my feet moved of their own volition until I stood mere inches away. I blocked his sun, casting a shadow over his ripped chest, and he glanced up.

His smile vanished as soon as the recognition dawned on his face. "Penny, are you stalking me now?"

"I…I didn't mean to." My attention flitted to the little girl covered in sand, who looked curiously at me. "I should go," I said. Feeling like an intruder encroaching on his time with his daughter, I took two steps back.

"You don't need to," he whispered. "Penny, this is my daughter Lucy."

With a wide grin, I sat down in the sand next to her.

"Hi," Lucy said, not stopping her task of filling her bucket with sand.

"Lucy, do you want to be the pretty princess who lives in the castle?" I asked.

She thought about it for a moment and glanced at her Dad. "No, this castle will be too small."

I laughed. "Then we better make sure we build it really big."

"Bigger than my daddy's house?"

"Hey now." Theo laughed, grabbing his daughter around the waist and tickling her down to the sand.

She squealed with laughter and I tried to remember why I was there.

What was I doing? You hate him, leave.

He handed over his yellow shovel as Lucy showed me the method of their building plans. We were building a castle with a huge moat around it.

She laughed and scooted in next to me as I dug out the moat. Theo sat across from me with his long legs criss-crossed, leaning back on his palms behind him as he watched us. I tried to focus on the moat and not the way his swim trunks rested just below a perfect v.

I took a moment to gaze at the tattoos on his chest and arm. An intricate ink pattern wove over his pectoral muscle and wrapped around his shoulder. The koi fish swimming up his arm, intertwined with the pattern.

It was sexy, and I wanted nothing more than to trace the pattern with my tongue.

What the hell, Penny? Stop.

Adoration filled Theo's eyes as he watched Lucy. *Was this the same man who taunted me daily?* I felt I was in the twilight zone.

"I have to get back to work," I said to Lucy, as I stood and wiped the loose sand from my shorts.

"Bye," Lucy said with a bright smile.

"Bye, sweetie."

"Penny." Theo hardly acknowledged me as I stood there saying goodbye to his daughter.

"Goodbye, Theo." I walked away without a second glance to him.

I felt his gaze on me the entire way back to the bar. It's funny how you know when someone's staring at your ass as you walk, and right now I didn't care. Let him stare. He would never touch it again. Or any other part of me.

Dex was the one I should want touching me. I tried to conjure images of his blue irises and dark, short hair. Nothing. The fact he was being so distant since he left town didn't sit well with me, and we needed to talk soon. I wouldn't put up with this shit from him. I must focus on my goals and not a boyfriend who didn't call and certainly not Theo Sullivan.

When I returned to work, I decided to take action into my own hands and stop letting the men in my life dismiss me.

I sat down in Theo's office and wrote him a note he would see tomorrow when I'd be off work.

I told him I wanted to set up a meeting for early Monday morning and would like to discuss all of the ideas I had for the Bearded Goat.

Maybe if I could get him alone, and he could see how serious I was, it would change his mind about promoting me.

I left him my number to text me if he agreed to meet with me.

Late Sunday evening, I received a text stating Monday morning was a go. Now I needed to woo him with my brilliance.

I was a nervous wreck for my meeting with Theo on Monday morning.

As I drove to work, my stomach a bundle of nerves, I gripped the steering wheel until my knuckles turned white.

I pulled along Ocean Drive and found a spot near the bar. It was early, the sun barely creeping up from the horizon, and only a few people were out and about. A few seagulls circled in the bright blue sky.

Even the vendors with their jewelry and t-shirt stands weren't fully set up.

A warm breeze blew off the ocean and swirled my hair around my face. Taking a deep breath, trying my hardest to gain confidence, I entered the bar.

Theo held his clipboard in his strong hands standing behind the bar when I stepped inside. He stopped, stared, and then returned his attention back to what he was doing.

"Hello," I said, nervously.

"Penny," he said, not looking up from the clipboard.

It felt eerily strange being in the bar alone with him.

I stood frozen as he laid the clipboard down along the bar and rested his arm over top of it.

His attention all on me, almost as if a fire was lit in his eyes, made me weak in the knees.

Moving wasn't happening, forget about breathing properly.

I cleared my throat and tried to speak, but the words wouldn't come.

"Are we going to start? Or are you going to stand there all day?"

Why was he only ever mean to me?

"No, we can begin," I said as I took a seat on a barstool with the wide oak bar between us.

"Ok, so start already. We have lots of work to do today."

Who was he kidding? It was Monday, and we would be empty all afternoon. But, I played his little game and smiled. "Of course. Well, I have some solutions to improve a few things around here."

"Continue," he snapped.

I could already see I had my work cut out for me this morning.

I opened my mouth to speak right at the moment he licked his full lips, and I stumbled over my words. "I think... we... could have theme days to drive in more business. Maybe Martini Mondays and we can run a discount on martinis."

He didn't move or acknowledge my idea so I continued, nervously. "And we could do Two-for-Tuesdays. Almost like a buy one get one free." I sounded like a child as I rushed the words out. Silence loomed between us. His dark eyes moved back to focus on his precious damn clipboard with no interest whatsoever in what I said. He wasn't taking me seriously and a fire ignited in my chest.

Who the fuck did he think he was? He could turn me on in a random club a few nights ago and now he couldn't even comment on what I said?

"Are you done?" he asked.

Was he for real?

"No, I'm not. You should listen to my ideas, Mr. Sullivan. They're good, and you don't have a clue what you're doing here." I could tell I crossed a line when his eyes snapped up to meet mine.

"Come here," he demanded.

Slowly, I slid from the stool, and walked around the bar. I didn't know what he wanted from me. Maybe to show me what was written on the clipboard?

"I'm here. Now what?" I asked with one hand on my hip, waiting for him to explain whatever it was he wanted.

"You think you're so superior, don't you?" He stepped closer, placing each hand on the bar, and enclosed me in his arms. I was trapped with nowhere to go as he leaned in closer.

My heart slammed in my chest as I tried to remember the question.

"Yes," I smarted off to him.

My chest rose and fell underneath my pink tank top. His eyes dropped to watch the action as I tried to step away.

"You think you're smarter than me?"

"Maybe a little," I breathed.

He was too close, way too close. He needed to back away.

"You don't think I can run this bar properly?" he asked, inching closer.

I tried to escape his muscled arms. "I don't."

"You're a fool. A stupid little girl who is mad about not getting her way."

"Am not," I said, sounding like the little girl he claimed. What was I doing?

"You infuriate me, Penny," he breathed across my cheek. His warm breath hit my skin and my nipples hardened instantly.

"You infuriate me more." A deep burning erupted in my core and I knew I shouldn't be feeling this way. I hated him.

"Why do you enjoy pissing me off?"

Me piss him off? Please. Oh God, is his dick pressing up against me?

The thought of his hardness pressed against me brought me back to months ago when he fucked me on the beach.

Both hands flew to his chest as I tried to push him away. As soon as they made contact with his firm muscles under his black t-shirt, they wouldn't move.

I could feel his heart pound vigorously in his chest, and I gazed into his eyes.

"If you would take me seriously, you would see I have a lot to offer."

His eyes narrowed as his brow furrowed. "Take you seriously? I *am* fucking serious. I want you gone."

"Gone?"

He wanted to fire me? For trying to improve The Goat? What kind of shit show did he plan on running?

"Yes, you piss me off, and I can't take it anymore." As soon as the words spilled from his mouth his lips collided with mine.

Oh, god, they feel so good.

His tongue thrust into my mouth and I sucked along the corners of his lips. My hands lowered to the edge of his shirt and I slipped my hand underneath to feel his warm skin on my fingertips.

With a flash, he broke the kiss. He grabbed at my shorts and dropped them to the floor. I stood there in my pink panties, and he growled at the sight.

"So fucking sweet," he moaned as he lifted me onto the bar.

He wrenched my legs apart as he slammed his face right into the spot I shouldn't want him most.

His nose and mouth pressed along the cotton of my panties as he nibbled on me through them.

The sensations were incredible, and I couldn't believe it when my hands fisted in his hair. My nails dug into his scalp as my head fell back along the bar. *Oh fuck. What was going on?*

In another quick second, my panties were being yanked down my legs and he threw them over his shoulder.

"This pussy drives me crazy. You fucking drive me crazy."

"You're an asshole," I said. Confusion took over as well as desire. Why did I feel this way? I shouldn't be enjoying this, at all.

I should tell him to stop, push him away. But, I enjoyed his tongue as it lapped at my wetness.

I rocked into his face as he growled against my clit. The vibration nearly sent me through the roof as he ate me like a man possessed.

He was relentless as he never wavered from my skin.

I should tell him to stop. Right. Now.

NINE

THEO

Her pussy tasted delicious, so fucking sweet.

The moment I tasted her sweet cunt, I couldn't stop. I wanted to fight with her, get her mad enough to hopefully storm out of the bar and never return, but my plan backfired when her hands pressed against my chest.

She smelled sweet, of coconuts and honey, and I wanted to know if the rest of her tasted as sweet.

It did.

When I pulled her shorts off, and saw her pink cotton panties, I lost it. My cock was ready and felt as if it could rip through my skin.

The only comfort would be inside her tight pussy.

The sight of her, open to me, and the way she tugged on my hair compelled me to please her.

What was she doing to me? Her pussy, god her pussy.

I slipped a finger inside and it gripped me, and I smiled along her skin. I held her clit between my lips and hummed gently as I flicked my thirsty tongue through her wetness.

Her hips bucked, and I clamped both arms around her thighs holding her in place. Sucking, and licking, I tasted the softness of her skin.

I returned my finger to her tightness as I tried to get my tongue inside her as well, pressing my nose into her clit.

A desire coursed through me, one I hadn't felt in many months.

The hypnotic smell of her drove me almost to insanity, and her moans pushed me further to the point of no return.

"Fuck, you taste so good."

I couldn't get enough. Her sighs and little yelps of anticipation made me want it even more.

Then, all at once, I shoved my whole face against her harder and harder. I rocked as she grinded.

She rode my face and I went fucking crazy.

She picked up her pace and I went even faster. She was hot, and so fucking wet. I loved eating her and went further inside her pussy with my tongue.

With her long legs holding my head in place, I delved deeper into her needy, tight cunt.

Her nails dug into my head as she tugged me closer. My pinky ran through her wetness and then I pressed it into her ass. She screamed my name again as she bucked against my face, and I couldn't wait to taste her orgasm on my tongue.

The smell of her overpowered me, the taste of her threw my system into a frenzy as I sucked along her dripping wet pussy begging for her release.

Eating like a starved man, I went deeper with my pinky into her ass. She was tight everywhere, and I fucking loved it.

The intensity of my mouth along her made my cock beat with pain. A pain only she could cure.

A pain so sharp, if I wasn't buried far inside her, I might never live through it.

"Theo, I'm coming," she cried, her voice holding a hint of familiarity.

A sense of pride washed over me knowing I'd brought her there. I was the sole reason she experienced something so powerful.

My cock yearned to be inside her, but I couldn't leave the position I was in. I didn't want to.

I was heady, my mind a fog of overloaded sensations.

She came all over me and I couldn't drink it up quick enough. I removed my fingers and grabbed her thighs, tugging her lower, crashing my lips to her.

I wanted her to taste how sinfully pure she truly was.

Her breathing was ragged, mine matching, and I sucked along her plush, full lips.

I broke the kiss and she smiled, and it almost ruined me. The flush of her cheeks, the swell of her breast and her body bare to me—I wanted her.

Her foot connected with my hip bone and she thrust her leg pushing me off her.

"Why?" she asked, hopping from the bar and scrounging around for her clothes.

I grinned, unsure what she meant. "What? Kiss you?"

"All of it. Why would you touch me like that?" she asked while crossing her arms over her heaving chest.

"You didn't like it?" I stepped out of her way while she buttoned her shorts.

"I...I...don't ever do it again." She tried to brush past me, but I stopped her with my hand gripping her elbow.

I couldn't concentrate with her around anymore, she needed to go. I acted a fool, and I wanted to stop my addiction to her—cold turkey.

"Penny, you're fired." It was time to be done once and for all.

Her expression ranged through a myriad of emotions. Beginning with shocked, ending in a fiery inferno of pure thundering rage.

Her cheeks turned a deep red, and a second later the palm of her hand connected with my face.

I dropped her elbow and leaned in close to her precious pouty lips. "Why the fuck would you think slapping me is a good idea?"

"You can't fire me."

"The fuck I can't. I'll say it again, you're fired. Get the fuck out." I was being tortured by her tight body, her soft lips.

"Why? For what reason?"

"For the reason I can't think straight with you around."

She laughed, and I cracked a smile. I was being fucking ridiculous.

"You're so hot," I whispered. *What are you doing to me?*

She looked at a spot over my shoulder, avoiding my eyes. "It *is* hot. They have fans you could install. I looked into it, they're cheap too."

Fans?

"I'll think about it." I moved away from her and grabbed my clipboard.

She narrowed her eyes.

"I said I would think about it and I will. Get to work...uh... *please*."

"Thanks." She smiled but it didn't reach her eyes. "Oh and Theo," she said softly when I turned away from her, "I'm sorry I slapped you."

"I'm sorry, too." I stalked away to my office, without looking back.

Once inside, I slammed the door and sank into my chair. Fuck, what happened—again?

There was something about her, something I couldn't escape.

The clipboard served as a stress reliever as I clutched it tighter in my hands. My cock throbbed and I took a few deep breaths.

Fuck, fans? I sat down and grabbed a pen.

Reasons to get fans

- The customers have been fanning themselves
- Might help keep customers in the seats, ordering
    - Penny seems to really want them
    - Her pussy tasted so fucking good

I hung my head, eyes closed as I took a deep breath through my nose. I struck my pen through the last line and continued.

- They'd probably be cheap
    - It's fucking hot
    - It would make her happy

Where was my brain? I ate out a fucking employee, on my fucking bar.

I was losing it.

Scrubbing my hand against my beard, I saw the mail stacked on the desk. The bold black letters of a name I knew all too well jumped out at me. Pardo Inc. I tore the letter open.

After scanning the words written on the paper, I crumpled the letter in my hand. A land developer wanted my oceanfront property.

Fuck, Dex.

I knew my asshole half-brother worked for Pardo Inc., and now they were all of a sudden interested in *my* bar? I pulled my phone from my pocket and called Xavier.

"Hey, Theo. How can I help you?" Xavier asked.

"Are you busy? I need to talk."

"Sure, what's up?"

"I got a letter from Pardo Inc. They're looking to buy the Bearded Goat."

"Hmm," he hummed.

"Well?" I snapped, pressing the phone closer to my ear. I leaned back in my chair. Xavier was always calm, and right now, I wanted to shove my fist through the wall.

"How's business?"

"Not good. I should have researched a little more before I made the hasty decision of buying this dump."

"Do you think Dex is behind this?" he asked.

"Absolutely. How could he not be? He's a fucking asshole. He always wants what's mine." My fist tightened on the crumpled letter. "What can we do?"

"Well, you could not sell to them. Pardo will stop at nothing though. You know how they are." He paused and I leaned up, rubbing my palm on my forehead. "The fuckers may even try to put liens on your building. They have deep pockets. They'll get you shut down in no time."

"Yeah, crossed my mind, too." I shifted in my seat as I ran my hand down my thigh, nervous energy careening through my legs.

"Do you think you could offload it?"

"I'm not sure there's another idiot quite like me who would buy it," I cracked a smile. "Maybe I should see what Pardo offers."

"Don't beat yourself up, Theo. I went over the paperwork with you. It appeared like a great deal at the time."

"Yeah, fuck little did we know. I invested a lot of money into this." I paused, my nervous energy dissipating, and let out a deep breath.

"Is there a way to drive more business? I mean your bar sits in the heart of South Beach."

"Yeah, but summer's coming." I leaned closer. "I've got this bartender and she gave me some great suggestions." Maybe it was the way I said it, or the tone of my voice, but he could tell more was at play.

"You're not fooling around with her are you?"

I blew out a breath, and rubbed the back of my neck with my hand as I tried to stall for time to answer.

"Jesus, Theo. Are you trying to give me a coronary? You don't need a sexual harassment lawsuit on top of everything else."

"I know," I said, shaking my head at my own stupidity. As bad as I wanted to never speak to her again, I still couldn't get the taste of her off my mind.

"Alright, first order of business, stop whatever is going on with her," he said firmly. "Next issue, keep her happy at work. No firing her. We don't need her to become a problem."

Ah, such little faith in me.

"Ok. What else?"

"If you think her ideas have merit, try them out. See if it helps. Maybe she has more." Maybe everyone did, and I should stop being the pompous asshole they pegged me for and listen to them.

"And as for Dex?"

"Let me see what I can dig up. Have you talked to him recently?"

"Not since the moment I caught him fucking Blair," I answered with a gruff voice.

I hated talking about Dex, hated thinking about him. He'd never even apologized for his betrayal. What a dick.

My other main concern was Penny. To make matters worse, I had to implement her ideas for the Goat. I finished my conversation with Xavier and headed off to Blair's to pick up Lucy for dinner.

With Lucy in the car, I knew I would need to make nice and call Penny.

"Lucy, want to go to dinner?"

"Yes," she giggled.

"Let's get you home first, and we can put on your pretty dress, ok?"

"Yes," she giggled louder.

With a quick rush into my condo, I dressed Lucy and pulled her hair into two pigtails. How would I be able to keep Penny happy at work. I knew what Xavier said was right. I'd need to make sure she didn't cause problems for me, although she didn't strike me as that kind of girl. As I grabbed my keys, I glanced at my clipboard from work, noticing the list I'd made previously.

- It would make her happy

I read the line a few times as I raked a hand through my thick hair. Lucy tugged on my other hand. "Ready, Daddy?"
"Yes, Boo. Let's go."
With one thought running through my mind, I locked the door behind us. *I really want to make her fucking happy.*

TEN

PENNY

Theo, Lord of the Pussy Eaters. What the fuck was I thinking?

Standing in the bathroom, staring at myself in the mirror, I couldn't look away from my guilt laden eyes. What the hell came over me? I thought of my boyfriend. My absent boyfriend. Was he really my boyfriend anymore? Was our relationship waiting for the official words to sever it?

My cheeks grew hot when I remembered the way Theo devoured me. Reaching out, I turned on the faucet and cupped the cool water in my hands, splashing my face. Never had a man go down on me in such a way before. He reminded me of what I read about in my romance novels. Except, he'd never say he wanted to drink from my sweet nectar. Not Theo. He'd say he wanted to eat my dripping, wet cunt. God, it was hot. It was almost as if he'd die a sudden death if he didn't taste me. I turned the tap off, took one last look at myself in the mirror, and knew what I had to do.

After my shift ended, I headed home in a daze riddled with guilt, doubt, and self-loathing. With a burst of anger, I grabbed my phone.

"Hello, Penny," he answered clearly annoyed.

"Why haven't you called me?"

"Been busy, babe." It was always the same thing, lately. How long did it take to call someone?

"Too busy to call your girlfriend?"

"Oh God, Penny, can we not get into this right now?"

"No, listen, we need to talk." A war erupted deep within my soul and I wanted to let it out.

"Can we talk tonight? I will call you when I get out of this meeting. Promise."

"Ok, but Dex, you'd better call." I wanted to end the whole thing right there on the phone.

"I will. Goodbye, Penny." He hung up before I could even get my goodbye out.

As I stared at it, it rang in my hand, making me jump. Theo's number displayed across the screen and I hesitated briefly, unsure why he would be calling.

"Hello," I said. It came out more like a question than an actual greeting.

Turning into my apartment complex, his sexy, deep voice sounded in my ear.

"Penny, I need your help." A hint of urgent desperation tinged his voice. "Can you meet me?"

I couldn't deny him anything at this point, I realized. "Sure, where?"

"I'm heading to dinner in a little bit with my daughter. Can you meet us at the Clevelander in about an hour?"

"Sure. See you then."

"Oh, and Penny, thank you." He let out a relieved breath, and I could almost feel its warmth through the phone.

"You're welcome. See you soon."

I raced inside to find an outfit to wear. It wasn't a date, he asked for my help. I needed to remind myself of this. Yet, why were my eyes checking out all the tiny dresses in the back of my closet? No, jeans and a cute blouse, nothing too fancy. I grabbed a flowy white cami and my most flattering pair of jeans. Just because I was helping, and not on a date, didn't mean my ass couldn't look amazing. I left my makeup soft and simple and ran a tube of peach lip gloss across my lips.

A little over an hour later, I strolled through the open courtyard of the Clevelander. The stark white building was in front of me, and my eyes swept the crowd out front searching for Theo.

"Hey," he said, standing behind me, tickling my neck with his heated breath.

In slow motion I turned to face him and was shocked by what I saw there—Theo, in a Star Wars t-shirt and black jeans, hand in hand with his daughter, her hair in pigtails. I wondered if he styled it. He smiled and looked a complete contradiction to the business badass I presumed him to be. Lucy smiled huge as she giggled her hello wearing a cute little green sundress.

"Nice shirt." I beamed at him. "May the Force be with you."

He grinned as his eyes lit up. "Thanks, I think so. Did you want to sit outside?" He led us over to the older woman behind the hostess stand.

"Three for outside, please," I said as Theo's hand landed on the small of my back. Tiny tingles sailed up and down my spine. He stood tall and towered over me with an easiness and laid back appeal I found tempting. I breathed him in, sex and sin floating off him in waves, as the woman led us to a table near the activity along Ocean Drive. The energy was magnetic--cars cruising the strip, valets rushing to park the Lamborghinis and other high-end cars, and people--people from all walks of life--everywhere, with the beach off in the distance. My eyes tried to take it all in at once.

We sat down, and he pulled out a small pack of crayons and a piece of paper from his pocket. Who was this man? A pack of crayons? My heart fluttered as I watched him lay everything out to keep Lucy occupied.

"I love it here," he said as soon as Lucy was busy coloring. "They have great food."

"Actually, I've never been here." His brows raised. "I know I know, it's unheard of considering the Goat is so close." I rested both elbows on the table and brought my hands to rest under my chin.

Theo leaned back in his seat. His brown eyes surfed over me as he rubbed a finger across his lips. "But, you're here now, so order whatever you like. This dinner is on me."

"Oh, I'll pay for my own," I said.

"Don't be ridiculous," he snapped. "I asked you here."

His smoldering eyes held mine in a mini stare off. Ok, I would let him pay for dinner. This was still not a date. People didn't bring kids on a date, right?

"Thank you," I relented.

Our server, an older man, with a dark tan and heavy accent, ambled over and to take our drink order.

"I'll have an Ice Tea, and a Shirley Temple for the princess. What would you like Penny? You should try their Miami Vice," Theo said.

"Ok, sure."

"Hope you're thirsty." His grin lit up his eyes.

"Why? I do know what a Miami Vice is."

"I know, but you haven't seen theirs yet. You'll see." He laughed, lightly.

"Oh, ok. Can't wait." I pointed to his shirt emblazoned with the logo over his chest. "Who's your favorite Star Wars character?"

"Obi Wan Kenobi," he answered immediately.

"Oh? Not Han Solo?" His answer surprised me. Most men usually liked Han, he was a jokester, and reminded me of Theo.

"Nah, don't get me wrong Han is great. But, Obi is the real hero."

"What do you mean?"

Theo placed his hands over Lucy's ears as he leaned in close to me. "He's the realest mother fucker in the whole saga, and he doesn't ever get any ass out of it. I mean he even does things as a ghost after he dies."

I laughed. "Oh, ok."

"Are you a fan?"

I shook my head from side to side. "Not really. I think I've seen maybe one of the movies."

"Blasphemy." He uncovered his daughter's ears as she smiled up to him. He kissed her on the top of the head as his boyish grin made another appearance.

The server arrived, and my eyes widened at the sight of the pink and white frozen drink in a glass as big as my head on his tray.

He set it down in front of me after handing off Theo's and Lucy's drinks to them. "Enjoy," the server said before walking away.

"It's going to take me weeks to drink all of this, lucky for you it's two of my favorite drinks combined." I grabbed the black straw and took a sip, savoring the coconut flavor on my tongue.

"Well, we have all the time in the world," Theo said, settling back in his chair.

The salty ocean breeze flew through my hair and the buzz of the cars driving by made me feel alive. "It's nice here," I said, opening the menu. Everything sounded delicious, and my mouth watered at the description of the hand-battered coconut shrimp appetizer. Theo tapped his fingers on the table.

"What?" I said, glancing up at him.

"It looks like you want to eat the menu. Hungry?"

I tried to think of the last time I ate. Lunch? Breakfast?

"Ravenous. I was thinking about the coconut shrimp appetizer. Mmm, it comes with a watermelon pineapple salsa."

He licked his lips as his eyes fluttered closed. They snapped open as he shook his head. "Is that all you're having? They have great pizza too. I usually get the double pepperoni. Check out the veggie pizza."

"Pizza," Lucy said as she bounced in her chair.

"You'll get pizza. You love pizza, don't you, Boo Bear?"

She nodded excitedly.

The waiter returned and Theo set the menu down. "Kids cheese pizza for the little lady. A coconut shrimp appetizer, and also a double pepperoni pizza, and a veggie pizza. Thanks." He handed the menus to the waiter and flashed me a devilish grin.

I squirmed in my seat under his scrutiny.

My attention was directed to the bright green crayon rolling off the table between Lucy and Theo's arms. Right when it toppled over the edge, Theo's quick reflexes snatched it right out of the air before it could fall any further.

"Great catch," I said, laughing as he took the crayon to color with his daughter.

He marked the page as he drew a few shapes on the paper. "Do you like to color?"

"Sure, when I was a kid I loved it. I haven't done it in years though."

He handed me the red crayon as Lucy's eyes grew wide, and I joined in their coloring.

"Here's a pretty flower," I said, drawing the petals as best I could.

"Ooh, I love it," Lucy said as she tried to replicate my flower.

"I used to love gardening with my mom when I was young." I let out a deep breath as memories of her flooded through me.

"What would the two of you plant?" Theo asked, looking up from his coloring project.

I glanced at Theo's strong hand guiding his daughter's tiny, delicate one, helping her trace a flower on the paper.

"Marigolds, Zinnias. Different flowers. We did have an orange tree and my father would pay me to pick the oranges for him." I smiled, remembering pulling the branches down to get the best ones. "He would give me a dime an orange."

He glanced up, cracking a grin as he set the crayon down. "What did you do with so much money?"

"Ha ha. Actually, there were quite a lot of oranges."

"I'm guessing you grew up in Florida."

I nodded as the waiter arrived with the shrimp and Lucy's pizza. He set them both down, and Theo picked up a knife, cutting small pieces of the pizza for Lucy.

I grabbed a shrimp, dipped it into the salsa, and brought it to my lips. It tasted like a slice of tropical paradise. The flaky coconut pieces danced along my tongue, and I closed my eyes to savor the flavor.

"I'm kind of wishing I was that piece of shrimp right now," Theo husked out.

My eyes sprang open at his words, and my cheeks flushed.

"Oh, sorry, these are really good." I picked up another shrimp and popped it into my mouth.

Awkward silence loomed as a black Dodge Viper pulled into the valet and parked. The door flung open, and a stocky man emerged, screaming in Spanish to the worker behind the valet stand. I snuck a glance at Theo and noticed he sat on the edge of his seat. The worker in the yellow jacket tried to calm the man with gold chains hanging around his neck.

Finally, the man handed off his keys and shouted, "Not a scratch on it."

"I guess he doesn't want a scratch on his car," Theo said matter-of-factly, relaxing back into his seat.

"Guess not." I laughed. "Why not park in the lot on the other side?" Theo shrugged his shoulders against a beautiful backdrop. Pink and orange colored clouds painted the sky as the sun set behind the Clevelander.

"What did you want to talk to me about?" I asked after a moment of silence passed.

"I wanted to talk about your ideas for The Goat and how we could implement them."

I wiped my mouth with the linen napkin and returned it to my lap. "Are you serious?"

Theo glanced to me after wiping the pizza sauce from Lucy's lips. "Yes."

Things had come full circle since this morning. I breathed in the circular moment in time as chills rolled down my back.

Finally, the recognition I deserved. "Ok, what did you want to start with first?"

"Let's start with what you were saying about the promotions for the days of the week. Tell me more."

We discussed all the marketing concepts for the days of the week promos while we devoured our meals.

Theo listened with interest as I spoke.

"I really think The Bearded Goat needs a new image. Look around," my eyes glanced up and down the neon lit strip, "everything here is all about class and pizazz. The Goat isn't a good fit."

"True, what do you think?"

"I think a whole makeover is in order. Maybe a new name, a new menu. Some fresh items would draw people in." He listened intently and my mind went blank. It was really hard to concentrate on anything other than the way his hair ruffled in the breeze, and the way the neon lights of the city cast shadows over his chiseled face. He was so approachable and carefree tonight. Like the night on the beach. I missed that Theo.

"This is great, Penny. I think it'll really help."

"Can I ask a question, Theo?"

"Sure, anything."

"Why the sudden change of heart?"

"What do you mean?" he asked.

"I mean, you hated the ideas this morning." I twisted my linen napkin in my lap.

"I didn't hate them, I was... preoccupied." He licked his lips, slow and sensual.

My face grew hot as the wicked gleam in his eyes reminded me of the shameless way he licked and sucked me until I came on the bar. He was The Lord of The Pussy Eaters, no doubt about it. With a pitter-patter in my heart, I pressed my thighs together and tried to look away.

"Fine, you didn't hate them."

"I didn't." His lips curved upward. "Are you busy later? I need to get Lucy back to her mother's, but I would like to keep discussing this."

"Sure, that would be great."

We finished off our entrees and left the restaurant.

"How about you meet me at the Bearded Goat and we can figure out a place to discuss things." He picked up Lucy and she rested her head on his shoulder.

"Sounds great."

I left him standing on the side of Ocean Drive and headed off in the direction of the sandy shore.

The moon hung low along the horizon casting a glowing reflection on the ocean. The waves were minimal, and I felt like a trespasser on a serene moment in time. My one-night with Theo, tucked away in the lifeguard station, flooded my mind. Tonight, I wanted to blurt out to him who I was. To hell with the consequences. But, I couldn't take the risk he would fire me, not now. My own dream was within reach. A wistful exhale left me and I closed my eyes letting the breeze rush over my skin. I could only hope I came out of this with my heart intact. Everything since the moment we met was one downward spiral into an endless abyss, and I was terrified no one would be there to save me. Or if I even deserved saving.

ELEVEN

THEO

Fuck yeah.

The plans Penny had were good, really good. She knew what she was doing. With a feeling things might work out in my favor, I drove Lucy home and headed to the Goat.

"Have you seen Penny?" I called out to Henry as I marched up to the bar he stood behind.

"Oh, we weren't expecting you this evening, Mr. Sullivan." His lazy surfer attitude annoyed me.

"I didn't plan on coming in," I said, scanning the open area for her. "Penny? Have you seen her?" I clipped off.

"Err…no, I don't know…"

"Think fast, I'm in a hurry."

"She's off tonight." With no patience to listen to information I already knew, I turned away and headed out onto the deck, my eyes still roaming.

As I stepped onto the faded wooden slats of the outside patio, the weight of seeing Penny off in the distance left me riveted. A blurred couple blocked my line of sight, and I pushed them slightly as they passed by.

Motionless, I confessed to myself—no matter how much I wanted to hate her, how much I probably could hate her; I didn't.

Her hair danced in the wind as the neon lights of the city outlined her sexy silhouette. My eyes wouldn't shift; my heart wouldn't beat—I couldn't focus on anything but her.

With a quick boost in confidence, I headed to meet her, trying hard to move my stoic feet. "Penny," I said, walking up behind her.

She didn't turn, she didn't move.

My heart pounded as she leaned her head back against my chest. She smelled good. She felt good.

Remembering where I was, I gently pushed her shoulders and she spun around. "Theo, hi," she whispered.

"Did you want to take a walk?"

"Yeah," she murmured.

We didn't speak again until we were well past the Bearded Goat, and the flashing lights of the main strip faded in the distance.

The air was balmy, yet she still held her hands clutching onto her shoulders. "You're not cold, are you?"

"No, just thinking," she murmured.

"Care to share?"

"You don't strike me as a father. The way you were with her tonight, it was sweet." She stopped walking to face me. "Well, you're not very sweet, Theo." She sighed, looking up at the sky, then back to me. "I guess I'm trying to figure you out."

"Ok, I don't really know what to say here." Her eyes bore into mine, and I felt as if she could see straight through the guarded fortress surrounding my heart.

"I'm just thinking out loud."

"I guess I'm not the pompous asshole you thought I was?"

"No, guess not." She smiled. "Where would you like to have this business talk?"

I tried to think of where to take her. "Why don't we sit on that beach bench over there?"

We sat side by side on the wooden bench perched near the coast, and I felt it was the time to "eat crow," as some say. "Tell me everything you think The Goat needs," I said, resting my arm along the back of the bench. "I had thought about a new name."

"Definitely." Her eyes lit up and I could see the passion shining from them. "A new name would be most important." She tucked a leg under her. "Also, you could do something with the patio. It needs help, everything is boring. New umbrellas, add more seating, some lights around the patio. Spice it up, add a little class to the joint."

I ran my fingers over my beard. "I like it."

"What would you rename it?" she asked.

"I was thinking of calling the bar, Lopa."

"I love Lopa, sounds very mystical," she said, as she turned her head to gaze out at the ocean. "Where did you come up with it?"

"Just a name that reminds me of something, and it's never really left me," I said, watching how the moon reflected against her skin.

She sighed as I slid closer. "It's a nice name. I think it will work."

I leaned in and ran my nose along her neckline.

"What are you doing?" she whispered.

"Shh. Quiet." My fingers were already running through her soft strands of gold. Her copper eyes glistened in the moonlight, and my eyes dropped to her mouth. Her lips called to me like a siren, and I would no longer deny myself the feel of them.

I joined our lips as her soft whimpers muffled into my mouth.

Her tongue slid along mine, soft and wet.

She broke the kiss suddenly and pushed my chest away.

Her eyes sprang open, and I couldn't read the expression hidden inside. "I still have a boyfriend," she said, softly.

My neck grew hot, my fingers still clutched in her hair as my mind raced. "Oh, ok. Then why are you here right now?" I breathed across her cheek.

"I'm sorry. I should have never let it get this far. You seem to always catch me off guard."

"Off guard?"

She pushed me the remainder of the way away from her.

"I can't think straight when I'm around you," she said.

I stood from the bench. "I understand. I'll see you tomorrow morning and we'll start implementing the changes. Have a good night, Penny." I clenched my fists, my knuckles turning white from the pressure.

She sat there with her mouth agape as I turned to walk away. I heard her faint goodbye as I neared Ocean Drive.

I pushed away any sexual desire toward Penny, as I slid into the leather seat of my Audi.

When I arrived home I grabbed my notebook and pen and tried again to write another list.

Reasons why you NEED to stop thinking about Penny

- She has a boyfriend
- She has a boyfriend
- She has a boyfriend
- She has a fucking boyfriend you fucking moron

With despair, I stared at the words written. I flipped the page, and with a new sheet I wrote out a new list.

Reasons why I CAN'T stop thinking about Penny

- She's everything I've ever wanted

Fuck. I slammed my fist against the notebook and tossed it across the room.

The next day I sat down in my office of The Goat to start the first phases of Penny's ideas.

First I needed a name for the project. I stared to the ceiling as my mind went blank. Grabbing my clipboard, I turned the page to a new sheet.

Plan of Attack

- Project Freckle's Ideas
- Operation Freckle's Brilliant Plans
- Penny may be smarter than me
- Freckle's sexy ideas
- Operation she has a boyfriend.

I stopped for a moment as the thought of her boyfriend hit home. *Fuck.*

- Project who cares about her (ideas)
- Operation Penny's bright ideas and stupid love life

- Operation this is fucking pointless

I give up. Her plan of attack would be just that. An attack I wasn't expecting. One which took me by surprise, freckles and all. Operation Fix This Bar and Leave Me Alone. I shoved the clipboard away from me and blew out a defeated breath.

After my failed attempt at a list, I called the fan company to have the oscillating fans installed.

Next, when Seth and Henry arrived, we spent the whole morning rearranging the patio furniture.

Penny suggested the patio could use a makeover, and more tables could be added to accommodate more guests.

Funny thing, the extra tables and chairs were in the storage room. The previous owner took them out because he didn't like the Feng Shui it created.

I, however, wanted to fill the seats, not harmonize with the universe.

A sign company to change the name was next on the list. After a quick phone call, the paperwork was taken care of to bring the Lopa to life.

Next, I went over a new menu with the head chef, Hector. We decided to serve sexy tapas as opposed to the fried, greasy garbage we slung out on a daily basis. As soon as I gave Hector the freedom to create whatever he wanted he came alive with enthusiasm.

His Spanish heritage had the small bites and appetizers appearing a lot more delicious than the previous menu.

The next day he made a few of the dishes and let the staff try the cuisine.

We dined on Ceviche, Ensaladas, and even Pulpo A Las Brasas.

Hector explained with a diverse menu of high-end tapas we would bring in a new class of guests, and this type of menu would showcase the Latin community of Miami.

The menu not only featured tapas, it also had family-style dishes of Paella, Albondigas, and Coctel Marino.

When Penny arrived, our eyes met, and I quickly squashed the feeling of rejection from a few nights ago and called her over to try some of the food.

"Try the Pulpo," I said, handing her a fork.

"Looks good. What is it?"

"Octopus." I laughed as her freckled nose turned away from the food. "It's good, I promise."

She was adventurous and I watched her try a small piece. "You're right. Hector, good job," she said, smiling to the chef in his white coat.

"Penny, can you help draft a few cocktail menus for the days of the week promotion in the office? Seth can handle the bar right now," I said.

"Sure. I'd love to."

She left down the hallway and I returned my attention back to Seth and Henry.

"Let's grab a few of the new chairs, guys. The installers for the fans should be here tomorrow or the next day, so it should be real nice out here soon," I said, surveying the back porch deck.

"Mr. Sullivan, it's real cool how you're trying to change this place to make it better. I think the previous owner only enjoyed partying and didn't care if this place went belly up," Henry said as he ran a hand across his jaw.

"You can thank Penny."

Thinking of her, I wandered down the hall to see how she was doing. I didn't want her to get too nosey in the office, or to see anything more from Pardo Inc.

I opened the door and she sat behind my oak desk, her bright teal tank showcasing her perky tits.

Shutting the door behind me, she lifted her head and her eyes met mine.

"How are the menus coming along?"

"Almost done. I'm excited." Her enthusiasm was cute. Her nose crinkled and the adorable freckles splattered there were highlighted by the sun coming in through the small window.

Upset about the idea of her having a boyfriend, I frowned as I moved closer to check out the menus she created.

Fuck, all of my emotions were centered around the anger I felt from the fact of the mysterious boyfriend. Did he eat her out as well as I did? I pushed away the thought of

Penny's succulent pussy as I tried to focus on the first set of menus.

The Spanish mosaic design she created along the paper was the perfect amount of class and not too girly.

She knew what she was doing, and I questioned why I dismissed the idea of her for the management job.

She stood from the office chair and came next to me to study the menus.

"This is really good work." I forced a smile.

"I think you need to advertise." Her eyes lit up as she spoke, her voice rising with excitement. "Maybe on the radio? Or the news stations."

Another great idea, and I fumed I wasn't the one who thought of it first. "Maybe."

"Oh come on. You know it's good," she taunted.

"I guess. I mean, meh."

She swatted my arm playfully as she laughed. "Ok, Mr. Tough Guy, I'll let you have it. You can tell everyone you thought of it." She chewed on the corner of her mouth as she glanced at me.

"No, I would never take the credit away from you. I'll admit it, Penny, you're the Queen of Good Ideas." I smiled and held up the menus as evidence.

"Why, thank you."

My smile faltered as I held her stare. The light buzz of the computer sang in the background, and my brow furrowed at the thought of the boyfriend once more.

I had questions, so many fucking questions. "Why?" was the only one I was able to mumble.

"Excuse me?"

We stood close as my heart thrummed. She was in my veins, and I couldn't master a thought around her. I wanted to fuck her against the desk, I also wanted to march out of this office and never see her again.

"Why did you let me touch you when you have a boyfriend?" I asked a little louder.

"I don't know," she whispered, her head bowing toward the ground.

"Fuck, you drive me insane." My hands flew to the sides of my head, tugging at the ends of my hair. I blew out a breath as she stepped closer.

"I never meant for anything to happen between us."

"But something did happen. A lot of things happened. I can't deal with this. You're my damn employee. I could get in a lot of trouble over you."

"Well, it wasn't *my* fault." She crossed her arms over her chest.

"It was *all* your fault, Penny."

Her eyes narrowed, brows furrowing. "Are you fucking kidding me? You came onto me."

Fury, red and molten, blinded me. I leaned inches from her face and whispered across her soft skin. "No other man's girlfriend should ever want me like you do."

Her hand connected with my face for the second time since I'd known her. She went to slap again, but I caught it right before she made contact.

"Stop."

"Or what? This time you'll fuck me?" she spat off.

"Watch what you say, I just might." I dropped her hand and slammed the office door behind me as I walked away.

TWELVE

PENNY

Did I hear him right? He might fuck me?

The sound of the office door slamming echoed throughout the small office as I stood there—heart pumping, body aching, and mind sizzling out of control.

Again, I asked myself, what the hell happened?

My body was drawn to him like a magnet, yet we were still unable to get along. Why was he so stubborn? Why couldn't he say thank you?

Last night at dinner, and even afterwards on the beach, I found myself opening up to him.

The whole time I was with Theo I'd never even checked my phone for Dex's call. It wasn't until I got home I saw the missed call from him.

No message, nothing. Just one missed call. One I demanded he make and then was too busy to answer.

I tried not to let it bother me as I gazed triumphantly at the menus one more time. Something I created was being implemented, and it felt fucking amazing. I wanted to make a quick call to my father and shove it in his face.

To show him I didn't need him or his money to make my way in this world. I was doing fine without him.

I returned to the computer and finished off the rest of the menus before leaving the office.

Walking out onto the patio I was amazed at how Theo managed to bring new life to the bar.

Sure it was little things—new potted plants on the deck, new patio chairs, umbrellas, twinkling lights that glimmered along the rails, and an overall sense of pride in the employees.

Now, I hoped my plans worked. They would. I'd been doing this since I was eighteen, and being twenty-six now, I'd say I picked up a few things along the way.

I spotted Theo standing in the corner of the patio, phone pressed to his ear as he ran a hand across his jaw through his beard. Gray clouds rolled off in the distance as the first drop of rain fell from the sky. A low grumble of thunder sounded from far away as Theo thrust the phone in the pocket of his khaki pants.

A gust of air flew past me as the storm picked up and was set to hit.

"Close the umbrellas," Theo called to Seth.

Together they worked to close the patio umbrellas before the wind picked up and tossed them. The rain fell in soft pellets at first but began to pick up in strength and ferocity.

"It's turning into biblical rain," Henry said, standing beside me.

As always with Florida, storms were a pain in the ass. It would rain for a few hours and then it would end until this time tomorrow when another storm would attack. I waltzed around to the opposite side of the bar and made a customer a drink.

A bourbon Manhattan. I plopped in the cherry and slid it across the oak bar as Theo walked up behind me—soaked.

He shook his hair, and the water droplets landed on my bare arms. "What are you doing?" The cold water brought a shiver down my spine as I wiped it away.

"What do you mean? I'm drying off," he said as he continued to run his hand through his hair, propelling water all over the place.

"What like a dog?" My temper flared, cheeks heated.

"Do I look like a dog to you?"

"The way you shake your head all around, you do." I crinkled my nose at him as a barely there smile broke across his face.

"Does it turn you on?" he asked, shaking his head over me. He laughed as the water from his hair rained down over me.

"You wish." I pushed him further away as someone clearing a throat behind us broke us from our fight? Flirting? Moment?

I wasn't quite sure what to make of what happened between Theo and me. He knew how to push my buttons, yet at the same time he knew how to make me laugh.

"Mr. Sullivan, there's a telephone call for you from a Mr. Chevy," Henry said.

Theo's expression changed drastically, gone was the laughter and playfulness, and in its place a sour mood took over.

Chevy? Dex Chevy? My Dex?

Did Dex know everything Theo and I did? Fingers shaking, nerves erupting inside me, I couldn't concentrate. I rushed to my phone hidden away in my purse and checked the display screen to see if I had any missed calls or texts—nothing.

With an uneasy feeling, I continued my shift as I served customer after customer.

After Theo returned from his phone call with Mr. Chevy, who I was still convinced was Dex, he wouldn't even look at me. Which made me more and more concerned.

I didn't want to ask, but the curiosity was killing me.

Before I had a chance to confront Theo, he left. At the end of my shift I packed up my belongings and headed out through the front wooden doors.

The storm all but dissipated, leaving in its wake a humid, muggy night. My hair frizzed to an ungodly mass of madness. I clutched my phone in both hands waiting until I was in my car to dial Dex's number.

Sliding into the front seat, I took a deep breath. After tapping the screen to call, I waited.

Nothing, straight to voicemail. Fucker turned his phone off. What was going on? I left the shortest message imaginable and headed home, defeated.

Whatever would happen, would happen—I felt I deserved it.

As I turned the corner of my street, I saw Dex's car parked in the driveway of my concrete block duplex.

He waited on the front porch steps, red roses in one hand—which I hated—and a box of chocolates in the other. He smiled.

"You know chocolate gives me hives," I said as I approached him.

His dark hair crumpled against his forehead while his blue eyes held mine.

"They do? I never knew." His answer was almost believable, except, I told him—probably more than fifty times at least.

"Why haven't you returned any of my calls? Why haven't you just plain called?" I wanted to fire off more questions but felt we should move our heartfelt reunion inside instead of on the front porch for all of the neighbors to see. He followed closely behind me to the kitchen.

"I was busy, Penny," he said as he tossed the flowers and chocolates on the island bar.

Picking the roses up with both hands, I brought them to my nose and took a whiff of their scent before plopping the arrangement back down on the marble counter in the same manner he had.

"Too busy for your girlfriend?" I challenged. There was no excuse for not calling, and I had every right to be pissed. He wasn't going to downplay my feelings again.

"I'm here now, so what's the difference?" He opened the chocolates and popped one in his mouth.

His arrogant attitude made me sick, and I wanted to flick his forehead. "What's the difference? Are you kidding?"

He'd changed from the man I once knew. Or did I ever really know him?

"Penny, calm down. You're getting worked up over nothing. I was with your father the whole time. Do you think I would cheat on you with your father looming off in the distance?"

I thought back to his "maybe" phone call with Theo and couldn't keep quiet on it. "Why did you call the Lopa today?"

"Excuse me?" He stepped back, suddenly seeming very out of place in my kitchen with his crisp-button down blue shirt and black pants pressed by a professional. I was sure even Dex's socks were cleaned and pressed by an expert. *Why was this guy my boyfriend? He was so charming when we first met. What happened?*

"The Lopa, you spoke to Theo Sullivan?"

"I know you work there, Penny," he said, crossing around the countertop to me, his expensive shoes barely making a whisper on the hardwood floors. "Your father and I are trying to acquire it. But, it's none of your concern."

"Acquire?"

He braced his hand on the countertop next to me. "Come on Penny, you're a smart girl. Figure it out."

My heart sank as I gazed at him. What did I ever find attractive about this man?

"Dex, it's over between us." Fed up, I walked away from him.

"What?" The word fell from his lips, and it almost sounded like he breathed it more than anything.

I turned to face him. "Did you really think I would stand for this?"

After an intense stare down, he snapped his eyes closed and then shook his head. When his eyes opened, his demeanor changed instantly, cold and calculating, as he stalked closer. "Don't think for one second I will stand for this. You're upset, so I will give you some time to really think about what you're saying."

"Of course I'm upset, but that's not why I'm doing this." My voice, devoid of emotion, drove my point home, "I'm doing this because I no longer care for you in the way you want me to."

He played with the button on his cuff as he smirked. "Fine Penny, I'm leaving now." His eyes swept over me. "Take some time to think. I'll be in touch."

Laughing to myself as he grabbed the box of chocolates from the counter, I watched him stalk off to his Mercedes. He peeled out of the driveway and sped off down the road.

I locked the door after he left and called him a few choice curses before heading into the bathroom to shower.

My mind drifted to Theo and how bad this was for him. My father and Dex would stop at nothing until they had the Lopa out of business so they could buy up the land.

I needed to speak with my father myself. It was past due we had a sit down.

I stepped into the shower and let the hot water work out the tense muscles in my shoulders.

Tomorrow morning, I would visit my father, first thing. But, for now there was only one person I wanted to see—Theo.

I phoned him, got his address, and raced to his house.

After he let me inside his swanky two-bedroom condo, I was met with beautiful floor-to-ceiling windows, overlooking Miami. His contemporary styled décor, with deep blues and soft greens, had a relaxing effect on my nerves. The place had a touch of class, yet it still felt lived in—a mahogany curio cabinet near the television caught my eye and I stepped closer.

"Are those dolls?" I peered at a Batman doll on the top shelf.

"Dolls?" His appalled voice sounded behind me. "No, these are action figures. Way manlier than a doll." He ran his hand over the box holding the Batman figurine inside.

"Oh, of course. I didn't mean to offend…"

"No, it's ok," he said, cutting me off, his eyes darting over the collection and unable to meet mine. "It's silly, really. But, I'm kind of a collector."

"It's not silly," I said, smiling. "It's actually kind of cool. So do you play with them?" I asked.

"No, Penny, I don't play with them." His gaze bounced to mine briefly before returning to his collection. "Actually, I don't even open the packaging."

"You don't open the packages? What a waste."

"Yeah they're worth more if they're never opened," he said, running his finger across his bottom lip.

"Oh, so you plan on selling them one day?"

He shook his head, cracking a smile. The boyish grin I loved so much made my heart race. "No, I'll never sell them."

I shook my head, grinning, as he asked me to take a seat on the deep-brown leather sofa.

"Thank you for seeing me so late, Theo."

"What's going on? Is everything ok?"

"Yes…no…I don't know." My mind overloaded with everything I wanted to say but couldn't articulate.

"Take a deep breath." He knelt in front of me as I closed my eyes. "In through the nose, out through the mouth." He placed both hands over mine on my lap. When my eyes sprang open they locked onto his chestnut-colored irises—so beautiful and intense.

"Better?" he asked as his thumb circled patterns against my fingertips. "Now start from the beginning."

"My father is Pardo Inc..." before I could finish, he muttered "Fuck" and stood.

Agitation radiated from him as he crossed to the large glass window and stared out. "Did you know?"

"That my father is trying to buy out the place I work at?" I rose from the couch as he turned away from the window and paced the hardwood floors in the large space.

He stopped, turning to face me. "Yes, Penny," he shouted. "Did you know?" His hand flew through his dark, disheveled hair.

"No."

"Fuck, I don't believe you."

"Excuse me?" I was pissed. What did he mean he didn't believe me?

"You heard me."

He stalked closer. I moved back. My knees hit the arm of the couch as he loomed over me.

"Back up." I tried to push him away but his body was solid, not budging as his chest pressed against mine.

"So, you came over here tonight to tease me? To throw it in my face that 'daddy' is trying to buy me out and you still have your precious boyfriend?"

My face grew hot. My body felt out of control. Anger pumped through me. And it was all more than I could handle.

His breath against my skin sent trickles of desire rolling through me. I wanted his touch, yet I fumed he could think so little of me.

"Think whatever you want," I said.

"Dammit, Penny." His eyes were as hard as his body as I tried to push him again.

My hands connected to his chest and my anger swelled. "You won't believe anything I say anyways, because you're the biggest asshole I've ever met."

His stubbornness was overwhelming. Losing all sensibility, I tried again to push him away. I was trapped between him and the couch, and he knew he had this control over me. I could see it in his wild eyes.

"I'm the asshole? Are you fucking kidding me? You taunt me while having a boyfriend." He was close, his lips mere inches from mine. I could almost taste his want.

"We broke up," I whispered before his hand fisted in my hair.

"Why?"

"Because I realized I held onto nothing and it wasn't what I wanted," I paused, staring into his eyes as they pleaded with mine, begging for my next reason, "and because I can't stop thinking about you."

"Fuck, baby," he breathed against my skin.

I was wet, instantly. A savage gleam flashed in his eyes as they feasted on my neck. I leaned my head back, letting him suck on my tender skin.

I want him.

Our breathing matched. Our hearts beat on the same thundering rhythm.

In a flash, he spun me around, his front to my back. I could feel his dick pressing into my ass. Clutching my hair in his tight fists, he controlled me as he grazed and nipped at the nape of my neck.

"Why do you do this to me?" he groaned.

He pushed me over the arm of the couch as he rocked his body into mine.

Oh fuck.

I'd never been so turned on in all my life. Pushing my ass out to meet his thrusts, he grinded against me.

The sound of my zipper reminded me how real this was as he lowered my jeans down my legs.

"Why do you make me so angry?" I asked as his gym shorts fell to his feet.

"I'm going to fuck you, Penny. I'm going to fuck all this anger away, baby." His lips were close to my ear as he moaned against it. My stomach pressed against the arm of the couch. He stepped back, and I could hear his harsh breaths.

"Theo, please."

I craved it.

THIRTEEN

THEO

I'm the only fucker who should be saying please.

Christ, the sight of her, bent over the couch. Her red satin panties, hugging her firm ass, nearly made me come. "Damn baby, you've teased me long enough. This ass," I grabbed a handful, "would look better with my cock in it." My fingers looped into the waistband of the material and slid them down her long silky legs. Fuck, she was gorgeous. "Red's my favorite color."

A wind chime sounded off in the distance as the air outside howled against the windows. My pulse thrummed in my ears as I ran my cock along her taut ass. She moaned, her back arching, and I stepped closer.

I ran my thick length through her wetness as the tip teased her entrance.

"This isn't going to be slow. Turn around."

"What are you doing?" She spun to face me.

"Wrap your legs around me and don't ask any more questions," I said, lifting her by the ass.

I carried her to the bedroom, slamming the door open. Throwing her on the bed, with nothing but her red lacy bra on, I fucking stared her up and down.

"Fuck, Penny, show me how filthy you can be."

Her cheeks blushed as she closed her eyes and her legs fell open. The sight of her glistening pussy made my mouth water. I remembered how good she tasted and wanted another lick.

"Touch your pussy for me, baby." I stood at the foot of the bed, gazing over her.

"Theo." Her fingers ran along her seam as she squeezed her legs together.

"No, keep your legs spread. I want to watch you touch your cunt for me."

"Oh, god," she moaned as her legs parted.

"How good does it feel? How wet are you?"

"Very."

"Yeah? Fuck your pussy with your fingers for me. Do it, Penny." I stroked my cock, abs clenching, as I watched her fingers enter her slick heat.

A low groan barreled out of me at the sight of her fingers slipping faster, in and out. I knew she was close when her moans escalated, the soft sounds driving my hips faster into my hand.

"Not yet, baby," I said as I climbed over her. Her eyes sprang open. Reaching down, I grabbed her hand, bringing her wet fingers to her lips. "Suck your fingers, Penny." Her eager lips closed around them and I leaned down biting a nipple through her bra.

Hungry for the tits spilling out over the top, I reached around to unhook the clasp and cupped each breast in my strong hands.

My cock throbbed painfully as I sucked a nipple into my mouth, gently biting the hardened skin between my teeth. Her back arched off the bed. I drove my thigh between her legs and could feel the wetness of her sweet pussy as she ground herself on me.

My heart raced when her hands skimmed down my sides, grasping at my hips.

I stuck a finger deep inside her, watching her face, as she bucked her hips off the bed. Her eyes met mine. "Fuck, Theo, I need to come"

I flipped over, lying on my back and pulled her on top of me.

She centered over my cock, sliding back and forth, but I didn't want her there yet.

"Grind your goddamn pussy all over me." I pulled her up my chest as she pushed her slick cunt along my skin. She grinded her way up to my face with my help guiding her all the way. "Ride my tongue, baby. Fuck my face, now."

"God, Theo," she murmured, "the things you say." She braced her hands on the headboard and soon I was surrounded by her needy pussy all around me.

This was my oasis.

I struck my tongue against her skin and slid it inside her opening. She rocked along me as I clamped my arms around her thighs to bring her closer to me.

Damn, her taste. I couldn't suck hard enough. I wanted more and more, greedy as she rode my face—I savored every minute of it.

"I'm coming," she panted.

I tasted her sweetness as it flowed over my tongue. Mmm, fucking nirvana.

Her legs shook on either side of my head, and I continued sucking until I knew she came down from her euphoric state.

She climbed off, but not before I grabbed her by the back of the neck and kissed her—hard.

"I need you right now." I'd never felt anything like it. She was all too compelling. I didn't know what would happen tomorrow, nor did I care. I knew right now I needed to be buried deep inside her, or I'd never recover.

Her eyes held mine as I let go of her neck, lowering my hands down to flick her nipple between my fingers.

"Ah, damn," she moaned as her head tipped back, mouth opening.

"Fuck me, you're sexy," I said as I rose on my knees and grabbed her ass with both hands.

I flung her onto her back. Her body like a fucking masterpiece fell to the bed, and I chased her down, smashing our lips together. I couldn't get enough. I couldn't give enough.

I grabbed a condom from the nightstand as her hand skated up her body, caressing her breast and squeezing her nipple.

"Theo, please fuck me," she pleaded as her golden hair splayed out across the pillow.

"Oh baby, I'm going to do a lot more than fuck you. I'm going to own that pussy." I rolled the condom down my thickening cock. Her eyes widened as she watched.

The anticipation of feeling her wrapped snugly around me was all I could focus on.

I moved myself to where I lay on top of her, my dick at her entrance. I entered her in one long thrust and her eyes slammed shut.

"Holy shit," she cried out.

I stilled a second as she acclimated to my size. She moaned and I dropped my forehead to hers. My mind went blank for a moment, not thinking, only feeling. She felt so damn good. Her silky pussy was something I only dreamed of.

I watched her face as she took all of me inside her. Rocking slow at first, I kissed along the corners of her mouth. "You're so beautiful," I breathed. Her body—so sensual, so desirable—belonged to me right now.

Her nails dug in, breaking skin as I picked up speed. My brain, a complete void of thought, acted out its primal instinct and rocked back and forth, slamming into her over and over.

She fucking felt just right.

"Oh, yes," she said again and again as my balls hit against her ass.

Gazing into her eyes, locking on them as my wicked cock took over, I became entranced by her. What was she doing to me?

"I want to come so deep inside you, make me...fuck, I can't take it."

Her heels dug into my ass, bringing me closer to her as I kept up my brutal pace. I never wanted this to end, but I could feel my orgasm looming just out of reach. I reached my finger down to play with her clit, snapping it between my fingers—once, twice, and for a third time before she cried out she was coming again.

Her eyes closed, and her face flushed with her orgasm as her mouth formed the perfectly shaped 'o'. I felt her, I fucking felt her.

Wrapping my arm under her knee, I brought her leg higher as I pushed into her deeper.

"You feel so good coming on my fucking cock," I groaned.

She leaned up and bit my shoulder between her teeth. I grunted as she clamped harder around me.

"Fuck, your pussy. I love it. I love your tight, wet cunt." I couldn't take it anymore, and my mouth pushed against hers as my orgasm shot through me like a freight train.

As my orgasm peaked, I gazed to the freckles along the bridge of her nose and brought my lips down to kiss each one.

After I came down from the high I found with her, our eyes met. Her questioning stare broke me as I leaned in and kissed her full lips.

I didn't want to pull out of her yet, knowing it would end. I had to be inside her for one moment longer.

"Do you think I'm an asshole?" I asked her, unsure of her answer.

"No." Her lips slowly, ever so slightly, lifted into a smile as I slid out of her.

I discarded the condom as she sat up.

"I'm sorry I didn't believe you," I said as I sat back down beside her on the bed.

"I'm upset too. I want to discuss this with my father. Maybe I can make him understand…" she trailed off as I grabbed each side of her face. Our lips met as a realization slammed into my consciousness—I really liked this woman.

She was smart, beautiful, and fucked like a goddamn legend.

We found our clothes as we made our way back into the living room.

It was well past dinner time and my stomach rumbled as I smiled to her. "Are you hungry?"

"Yes, starved."

I ordered Thai from a place not too far from my condo.

"Tell me about your father. Does he know you work at the Lopa?" I asked as she raised her legs to rest them on my lap.

"He does. He wants to control my life further. If he can get rid of the one thing I love, then he knows he's won. It's the reason I didn't want to be associated with him anymore. I didn't want him to rob me of the memory of my mother. It's the reason I took her maiden name after she died," she said, playing with a strand of her hair between her fingers.

"You love the Lopa?"

"Of course I do," she said with a sparkle in her eyes.

"It makes me feel better knowing you care so much. I guess when I bought it I figured no one would love it as much as I do. Does that make sense?" I leaned back into the couch and pulled my feet up onto the coffee table.

"What about you? What made you want to buy a bar?" she asked.

I took a deep breath before beginning, "When I was a kid we didn't have much. My mother tried hard for us. My father was a deadbeat dad, and my mother was a single mom trying to raise my brother and me." I cleared my throat before continuing, "My mother on the weekends would sell jewelry she'd make along Ocean Drive. My brother and I would play on the beach, or we would run down and peer into the windows of the closed clubs. We wondered about everything that happened when the city came alive at night."

"Right," she weighed in.

"There was a man, he would always buy us an ice cream cone from the vendor near my mother's booth. He was a bar owner, and everyone loved him. He ran South Beach in my eyes, and I remember wanting to be like him. I don't know, from there it kind of escalated and I wanted it more and more. Silly, huh?"

"No. It makes me happy you love the Lopa, too. I think with all the changes you've made; it should be great there once again." She drew her knees to her chest as she wrapped her arms around them.

The doorbell rang, and I sprang from the couch to grab the order.

I brought the food to the counter in the kitchen and we rummaged through the bag.

"Hey, don't take all the spring rolls," she said, laughing, as I grabbed a few.

"I got you Pad Thai. Thought that would make you happy." I winked as she laughed harder.

"That's one of the things."

I tilted my head at her, suddenly wondering what things made her happy. "What else?"

"Turtles," she said, picking up a roll and closing her lips around it.

Watching her mouth close around the roll turned me on and made me ready for round two.

"Why turtles?' I asked, opening the containers.

She sat down on a stool at the counter, and chewed her lip for a moment before looking up at me. "Well, my mom used to tell me a story when I was a little girl about a magical loggerhead sea turtle." She looked away from me and toyed with the noodles on her plate. "The loggerheads are huge, and this mystical turtle was the biggest and wisest one of all.

The turtles would travel all over the world to find the perfect spot to come ashore to lay their eggs. When the babies hatched, somehow, they always made their way back to their mothers. So, she said the turtle watched over all the baby turtles guiding them safely home. She also said the loggerhead would protect all children—human or animal—and would always help guide them home to their mothers."

I smiled wide and sat down beside her. "Ah, I know all about making up fairy tale shit for kids."

She laughed. "Well, I like to believe what she said." She paused and looked over at me. "When she died, I always found myself associating anything that was a baby sea turtle with her. Hoping one day I would make my way through the great big ocean of life and find my way back to her."

I turned to face her and pulled her stool in closer to me. "I'm so sorry, Penny. I didn't mean to make you sad."

She shook her head at me. "No, it's ok. The turtle makes me happy." She smiled and rested her cheek in her hand. "I collect some, because it makes me feel like she's here with me, you know? Watching over me. It's why I got this." She turned and brushed her long hair off of her shoulders revealing the nape of her neck. A tattoo.

My fork clattered to the countertop.

A tiny sea turtle.

FOURTEEN

PENNY

Why is he staring at me like I opened one of his dolls?

"Are you ok?" I asked. Theo hadn't uttered a word since I showed him my tattoo.

It freaked me out the way his eyes were fixed on me.

I hopped down from the stool and closed up my container of noodles. "Cat got your tongue?" I picked up his fork he dropped and he grabbed my hand.

"Penelope," he whispered, sending chills skating through my body.

He never called me by my given name, and for a moment I saw the recognition in his eyes.

"Yes."

"It's you," he muttered, stepping closer.

I nodded. "It's me. Are you ok?"

"From the beach?" His eyes pierced straight through me, letting me know he remembered.

I didn't know what to say. I dropped the fork as he pulled me tighter against his body.

He tipped my chin with his finger and his eyes spoke to mine in a silent plea to answer him.

"Yeah, from the beach," I said, barely audible.

Suddenly, he kissed me. Our tongues collided, racing to get closer, rushing to feel each other.

He slowly broke the kiss and stepped back. "I have so many questions."

A tingling sensation shot through me and my neck heated which was in direct correlation to my pounding heartbeat.

"Ok."

His vulnerability shone in his eyes as they searched mine. He raked his fingers through his wild, messy hair as he took in a deep breath. "Why did you leave me?"

My heart fell as I remembered. "Work. I actually got fired that morning."

"I'm sorry." His voice was still soft as if he couldn't believe I really stood there.

"It's ok. I came back and you were gone." I wanted to tell him I thought about him many times since our fateful night. But, his reverent stance caught me off guard. Was he mad?

"The first day at the Goat, did you know it was me?"

"Yeah," I whispered. His eyes flickered with something which scared me. Not anger, disappointment.

"Why didn't you tell me?"

"You didn't recognize me. I didn't know what to think."

"I'm sorry, you should have told me."

"I thought you would fire me, and I needed the job." I turned away and played with the box of noodles.

"Fire you? Fire you for what?" He stepped closer, running his hands down my arms.

I turned and met his questioning eyes. "You weren't very nice when we met, Theo."

"Do you know why I chose the name Lopa?"

"No."

"I didn't forget you." He paused and unknowingly took another piece of my heart with his next words. "Lopa is a form of the name Penelope."

Relief swam through my system as I realized I wasn't some one night stand he had a million times. The Lord of my O's didn't forget me, he thought about me too.

"I almost feel jealous of myself," I joked as a smile spread across his handsome face.

"You have no reason to ever feel jealous of anything." He gripped my hips with both hands and pulled me closer. "You've been a part of me since that night, and I was never able to let you go. I have you now, and you can bet your fucking life I won't lose you again." His eyes swept over me as a lazy smile appeared.

God, this man is sexy.

"Theo, you never really left me either," I whispered.

He closed his eyes letting my words sink in. When he opened them a bit of mischievous fire blazed. He kissed me, pressing his hands under my ass lifting me up. Passion, want, and pure lust pulled me under like a rip current until I was drowning in the way he made me feel. My legs wrapped around him as he carried me down the hallway.

"What am I going to do with you, Penelope?" he whispered across my lips.

"Make me feel everything."

And he did. He touched my body in ways I'd never felt before, ever. All night he kissed every part of me as I gave him more pieces of my heart.

When he pumped inside me, I'd never been more connected with any man before. It was scary and exhilarating all at the same time.

And when I lie in his arms, and the lull of sleep threatened to pull me under, I felt Theo's lips press against the tattoo on my neck. I fell asleep with a contented smile on my face and prayed it would never go away.

The next morning, I met with my father.

I left his office despondent.

FIFTEEN

THEO

Reasons Why I Need Mr. Pardo's Help

- I'm fucking broke
- Seriously his proposal isn't too bad
- I'll still get to be part owner
- If I don't he'll shut me down and I'll have nothing

Fuck, this was hard. I contemplated my options as I sat at the Hard Rock Cafe in Bayside, near downtown Miami. I glanced at the beverage napkin on the table as I jotted down my options for even considering Mr. Pardo's proposal.

- If I agree maybe he'll see how serious I am about Penny
  - I can't be broke and take care of her
  - I need this to work
  - I can NOT fail
- Xavier thinks it's my best option
  - What other choice do I have?
  - I need this to work for Penny

I heard the sound of a throat clearing and crumpled the bar napkin in my hands. Turning my head, I stared at a bald, squat man with the same color eyes as Penny.

"Theo Sullivan," he said as he took a seat at the table.

"Mr. Pardo, I'm presuming."

"You presume right. Have you read over the contract I sent you?" His long fingers weaved together along the table as his eyes roamed over me.

"Yes, and I've signed it." I handed over the agreement.

The cacophony of music and chatter was overwhelming, and I couldn't think clearly. I loosened the Windsor knot of my red Hugo Boss tie and flagged the waiter. He stopped by, and in a daze I ordered a drink, a stiff one.

"Relax. Everything is going to work out great."

"So, how will this work exactly?"

"I want to make sure my investment is taken care of properly."

I narrowed my eyes, grinding my teeth together. "Yes, what do you have in mind?" I was at this man's mercy now; my own decisions didn't matter.

"I'm bringing in someone very experienced to run the bar," Mr. Pardo said, amused by himself.

"A new boss," he boasted as he smoothed over the material of his button-down, dress shirt.

"Who?"

The music changed to "Black Magic Woman" by Santana and I spotted Penny across the restaurant. She was beautiful and she stole my breath away.

It all kicked in slowly, an arm wrapping around her from behind, my breath catching in my throat, and my brother's triumphant smile shining down on her.

Our eyes met for a second before she returned her attention to Dex.

I turned and saw her father beaming at the two of them, and my heart plummeted to my stomach. They made their way to the table, together. Holding hands like a fucking couple. What the hell was going on?

"Ah, there's my daughter and her fiancé now."

Fiancé?

"This is the new boss...Penelope."

To be continued…

BEARDED GOAT COCKTAIL MENU

Cosmopolitan-
3.25 oz of Tito's Vodka, ½ oz of Triple Sec, and cranberry. Shake Vigorously. Serve up in chilled glass. Garnish with a lime.

Manhattan-
2 oz of Rye or whiskey, ¾ oz sweet vermouth, a dash of bitters garnished with a cherry. Serve up in chilled glass or on the rocks.

Malibu and Pineapple-
A generous pour of Malibu Rum, add Pineapple Juice. Served on the rocks.

Blow Job Shot-

Pour ½ oz Baileys, ½ oz Amaretto, and ½ oz Kahlua into a shot glass. Top with whipped cream. Remember use no hands when swallowing it down.

Miami Vice-

A Blender is required. This drink combines a Strawberry Daiquiri and a Pina Colada. ½ of each drink in one glass. Recipes Below.

Pina Colada-

A Blender is Required. Malibu Rum and Pina Colada Mix into a blender with plenty of Ice. Mix on High. Pour and enjoy.

Strawberry Daiquiri-

A Blender is required. Lots of Rum and Strawberry Daiquiri Mix into a Blender. Mix on High. Pour and Enjoy.

Play List For Like A Boss

Jimmy Buffet's "Cheeseburger in Paradise."

Kodaline "All I Want."

Andrew Belle "In My Veins."

Santana "Black Magic Woman."

Seafret "Oceans"

Keaton Henson "Small Hands"

BAR SONGS

"Piano Man" by Billy Joel

"Hotel California" by The Eagles

"Don't Stop Believing" by Journey

"Come Sail Away" by Styx

Follow my complete playlist on Spotify:
https://open.spotify.com/user/sunshinekiddo/playlist/4zLXVwjZrpHmpY3Bz8gu59

If you follow along in the Brothers Chance Playroom then you know what's coming next. I have two lists which have taken me a long time to compile.
These are things I do when I am not writing. Little lists I come up with.

I know what you're thinking, I am crazy. But just wait it gets SO much worse.
Here's a list of other words for the male penis.

Adolph
Albino Cave Dweller
baby-arm
baby-maker, baloney pony
beaver basher, beef whistle
bell on a pole, bishop
Bob Dole, boomstick
braciole, bratwurst
burrito, candle, choad
chopper, chub, chubby
cock, cranny axe, cum gun
custard launcher, dagger
deep-V diver
dick, dickie
ding dong mcdork
dink, dipstick
disco stick, dog head

dong, donger, dork
dragon, drum stick, dude piston
Easy Rider
Eggroll, Excalibur, fang
ferret, fire hose, flesh flute
flesh tower, Frodo, fuck rod
fudge sickle
fun stick, gigi, groin
heat-seeking moisture missile
hog, hose, jackhammer
Jimmy
John
John Thomas
Johnson
Joystick, junk, kickstand
king Sebastian, knob
lap rocket
leaky hose, lingam, little Bob
little Elvis, lizard
Longfellow, love muscle, love rod
love stick, luigi, manhood
mayo shooting hotdog gun, meat constrictor
meat injection, meat popsicle, meat stick
meat thermometer, member
meter long king kong dong
microphone, middle stump
Moisture and heat seeking venomous throbbing python
of love
Mr. Knish
mushroom head

mutton, netherrod
old boy, old fellow, old man
one-eyed monster
one-eyed snake
one-eyed trouser-snake
one-eyed wonder weasel
one-eyed yogurt slinger
pecker, Pedro, peepee
Percy, Peter, Pied Piper
Pig skin bus, pink oboe, piss weasle
piston, plug, pnor
poinswatter, popeye, pork sword
prick, private eye, private part
purple-headed yogurt flinger
purple-helmeted warrior of love
quiver bone
Ramburglar
Rod, rod of pleasure, roundhead
sausage, schlong
schlong dongadoodle, schmeckel
schmuck, shmuck
schnitzel, schwanz, schwartz
sebastianic sword, shaft, short arm
single barrelled pump action bollock yogurt shotgun
skin flute, soldier
spawn hammer
steamin' semen truck, stick shift
surfboard, Tallywhacker
Tan Bannana, tassle
third leg, thumper, thunderbird 3

thundersword, tinker
todger, tonk, tool
trouser snake, tubesteak
twig (& berries), twinkie
vein, wand, wang
wang doodle, wanger
wee wee, whoopie stick
wick, wiener, Wiener Schnitzel
willy, wing dang doodle,
winkie, yingyang, yogurt gun

Here's the Vagina List
Please don't hate me. Ha. (some have been removed)

1. 2. 3. Bearded Clam 4. Vagina 5. Soft Shelled Tuna Taco 6. Camel Toe 7. Slit 8. pit 9. Cum Dumpster 10. Fuzzy Taco 11. Air Pipe 12. 13. Beaver 14. Tuna Town 15. Punani 16. Puntang 17. ECD 18. Sweaty Love Box 19. Coochie 20. Stabin' Cabin 21. Muff 22. Peach 23. Snake Pit 24. Holster 25. Snatch 26. Chonch 27. Pinoché 28. Hatchet Wound 29. Stinky Pink 30. Moose Knuckle 31. Small Aquatic Animal 32. Fetus Factory 33. Pudunda 34. Arm Sleeves 35. Finger Warmer 36. Bottle Holder 37. Anal Alternative 38. Susan 39. Land Down Under 40. Joy Trail 41. Tunnel of Love 42. Crotch Sink 43. Sex 44. Nappy Dugout 45. Fur Pipe 46.

Flitter 47. Dinner 48. Meat Tunnel 49. Hole 50. Gash (Bleeding) 51. Roast Beef 52. Penis Coffin 53. Flower Bud 54. Pin Cushion 55. Velvet-Lined Meat Wallet 56. Cooter 57. Fur Burger 58. Fuzzy Credit Card 59. Pee-Pee 60. Miss Flappy 61. Mr. Happy's Flappy Garage 62. Texas Tunnel 63. Front Butt 64. Penis Fly Trap 65. Red Snapper 66. Trouser Trout 67. Panty Perch 68. Box 69. Money Maker 70. Sideways Smile 71. Hair Pie 72. Abyss 73. Black Hole 74. Skirt Scampi 75. Beef Curtains 76. Funnel 77. Cherry Pie 78. Cherry 79. Penis Warmer 80. Microwave 81. Womanhood 82. Mace 83. Fat Fold 84. Split Tail 85. Female Genitalia 86. Jiz Creek 87. One E One Horned Flying Purple Penis Eater 88. One E Monster's Cave 89. Sheath 90. Plump Pink Penis Cushion 91. Hot Pocket 92. Cum Muffler 93. Weiner Wagon 94. Weiner Getter Wetter 95. Pink Void (get it?) 96. Pink Penis Caddie 97. Cum Sponge 98. Cum Catcher 99. Mound 100. Moist Monkey Mauler 101. Devil's Ditch 102. Pike Purse 103. Quarry 104. Carp Carnival 105. Fish Farm 106. Skinner 107. Hole 108. Slime Well 109. Humpadelic Hymen 110. Can 111. Tampon Tamer 112. Daddy's Dead End 113. Pink Room 114. Penis Receptacle 115. Oval Office 116. Flapper 117. TLU 118. Lasagna Lips 119. Bean 120. Hallway 121. Panty Puppet 122. Tuna Melt 123. Penis Garage 124. Ball Backboard 125. Porch 126. Yeast Factory 127. Yeast Infection Connection 128. Chatterbox 129. Box-on-the-Jack 130. Limpy's Hump Palace 131. Pinochtitlán 132. Meatball Sub Tub 133. Tub 134. Fertilization Plantation 135. Park & Ride 136. Slip & SLide 137. Love Muffin 138. Hawaiian Hairball 139. ilocks and the Three Hairs. 140. zilla 141. Cubby Hole 142. Semen Locker 143. Apron 144. Bone

Collector 145. Grassy Knoll 146. Fancy 147. The Mouth 148. One E Al's Beef Corral 149. Duck Billed Fatapuss 150. Rubber Rimmed Romper Room 151. Masturbation Contingency Plan 152. Tar Pit 153. Sock 154. Pelvis Furby 155. Sperm Jacuzzi 156. Horny Harry's Hobby Hole 157. Knuckles 158. Ho Chi Minh Trail 159. Yellow Prick Road 160. Great Red Ravine 161. Holiest of Holies 162. Penis Piñata 163. The Other White Meat 164. Baby Vending Machine 165. Toothless Grin 166. One Eye's Wonder Hole 167. Purple Headed Party Shack 168. Penis Parking Lot 169. Pimp's Paycheck 170. Glory Hole 171. Uteran Hatch 172. Watertight Door 173. Horny Halo 174. Gonorrhea Gainer 175. Tinkle Bird 176. Chlamydia Canal 177. Right Of Passage 178. Long Wanger Hanger 179. Pretty Little Penis Purse 180. Snuffleufapuss 181. Trophey Recepticle 182. Main Vein Drain 181. Pink Penis Pooker 182. Purple Headed Pit Stop 183. Spunk Bucket 184. Organ Formally Known as 185. Port of Entry 186. Errection Correction Trench 187. ECF 188. Clit Crate 189. Royal Envelope 190. Eager Mating Canal 191. Lunch Box 192. Inni 193. Velvet Underground 194. Big Berthat 195. Cooze 196. Quim 197. Extremely Durable Penis Orifice 198. Fun Bag 199. Lovin' Oven 200. Penis Slide 201. Pride Land 202. Crank Case 203. Douche Caboose 204. Sausage Delivery Orifice 205. Clam Flavored Pothole 206. Nut Cam 207. Mama Joe 208. Next to the Butt Nut Hut 209. Pot Pie 210. Fuzzy Grape 211. Buried Treasure 212. Shrimp Bed 213. Cozy 214. Warm Apple Pie 215. Honey Pot 216. Bloomin' Onion 217. The Q 218. Pee-Wee Grinder 219. Bloody Mary 220. Furry Flounder 221. Bald Eagle 222. Chang-Chang 223. Whisker Bisket 224.

Muscle 225. Rabbit Hole 226. Snoop Nappy Snatch 227. Hairy Dime Slot 228. Skanky Hood 229. Landing Strip 230. Shaft Alley 231. Cunny 232. Kiki 233. Church Box 234. Sperm Bank 235. Meat Drapes 236. Misty Crevice 237. Knuckle 238. Snake Ranch

Congratulations

You've made it this far. Just a little bit more to go. Let me thank a few people.

A few things about me you should know. I am a list lover, and thought long and hard about making my acknowledgements into a list of sorts.

Before I do that, I want to tell you this part of the book is NOT edited, I'm writing it really quick and then will probably never read it again.

I got the idea to write an erotica novel while sitting around with my brother and cousin, Cara. She told us we needed to love on a certain well-known book and my brother, Jacob and I read the book. We each even liked it, and thought we want to do this.

So together we decided to give it a shot.

I thought about what type of story to write. And, to be honest the title of the book came to me before anything else. So I went with it. I picked some character's names, and I wish I had a cool story of how I found their names, but I really don't. Just picked some names out of the air.

Now I do have to say, I started writing and got 23 thousand words into the story and hit a wall. And scrapped the whole thing and started fresh. I felt it was a good move, the first book I kept running into babysitting issues and let's face it Penny wasn't painted in the best light.

Love A Boss is the sequel and will be releasing very soon. To make sure you don't miss this release, I've made it easy to stalk me.

[FACEBOOK](#)

[TWITTER](#)

Instagram: https://www.instagram.com/loganchance85/

Jacob and I also have a naughty playroom which is tons of fun and we are always accepting new people.

You can join [here.](#)

All right I have a bunch of people to thank and I guess I should start with my brother, Jacob. Thanks. You've always had my back and you're more than just my brother, you're my best friend.

When Jacob and I opened our Facebook account, we had no clue as to what we were doing and there were a few who helped us. They took us under their wings so to speak.

Paula Dawn found two brothers goofing off and helped us navigate our way.

Diane Hamilton- our personal assistant, who really has her work cut out for her. She keeps us in line. She helps us in every way possible, from booking our takeovers, spotlights and such. She is very organized which helps offset our very unorganized ways. Diane thank you for everything. You are truly special, don't ever think otherwise.

She also runs our street team 'The Chance Takers' which is a great group of girls dedicated to helping us get our names out there. They work long hours to share our teasers and enter us into contests. Thanks girls, The Chance Takers--Donna Benton, Kerry Callaway, Brittany Danielle Christina, Elena R. Cruz, Lisa Davall, Paula Dawn, Kaye Spingett, Beth Hurley, Rhiannon King, Val DeGeorge, Karen Dillon, Jessica Green, Misty Paige, Miriam Meza, Michelle McKenzie, Laurie Davis, and Ely Darcy. You girls amaze me every day. And I am honored to call you ladies my friends. Thank you.

To all the girls in the Brothers Chance Playroom, you girls make everyday fun. I've had a blast and love the inside jokes we've come to laugh over. I don't think there is any type of food we can look at the same anymore. You ladies make me laugh, and thanks for the tags in all the Star Wars memes. I'm glad we were able to bring together a great group of girls who value friendship and support in one another. Thanks for believing in us.

Thank you to Jessica Hildreth in an amazing book cover and smokin' hot teasers. You have a great eye for detail and a vision to know what looks amazing. You really are a top-notch professional.

Valerie DeGeorge, a woman who has become such a great friend. A little New Yorker in Florida. Val, I cherish our friendship and hope you don't get too mad when I just go a whole day of saying nothing but, lol, thanks, or nice. I may not be a talker, I guess I'm a better writer. Always remember you deserve so much more.

Jessica Green, the woman who made the claim she was my number one fan from day one and has never let me down. You are definitely my type of weirdness and always a ray of sunshine, you truly are a wonderful person. Don't ever forget it.

Laura Martinez, I have to say in the beginning I sure didn't know what to make of you. But, I'm glad we were able to get to know each other and you have become a great support to Jacob and I. I truly do appreciate all you do for me. You're definitely my favorite little spitfire.

Denielle Hoppe, thank you for grabbing us in the beginning and we really have learned a lot from you. Sorry for sometimes being impossible and making you chase me to answer a simple question. One day I'll be able to manage my inbox.

Vivian Freeman, thanks for being a pain in my side, and for always offering up a side of sass as well. I'm glad you've gotten used to my one word answers. And thanks for all of your help on this book. And of course thanks for opening my eyes and helping to veer me through this Indie World.

For My Beta Readers
Jessica and Valerie, you're input and dedication to my success will be valued for many years to come.

Dawn Costeria and Angela DeMarco, you two have been nothing but amazing and helpful with every bit of assistance you've offered. I thank you both for everything.
Dawn, your help on this book was outstanding and I am so grateful for you.

Donna Benton, thank you for all of your notes on Like A Boss and addressing the issues of Theo and also you've been a great help getting my name out to the masses. Thank you.

Louisa Brandenburger, thanks for reading the very first scene of a story that was scrapped. I'm glad you were able to help read the final and thank you for your words of wisdom.

The Blogs, without book bloggers we would be nothing.
A big shout out to these blogs for all of their help and guidance.
Dirty Laundry Review, Amo and Sarah's Book Corner, Divas Book Lounge, Blushing Babes Are Up All Night, Vox Liberia, Jackie & Val's Book Reviews, Beaute De Livres, The Bashful Book Whore, Book Lover's Hangout, Sassy Book Club, Amazeballs Book Addicts, and many many more.

To all of the blogs who have helped spread the word of the Chance Brothers.

Paula Dawn, thank you first and foremost for all of your tireless efforts working on my book. Your dedication to every sentence in this book resonates in me, and I will never forget it. You helped bring Penny and Theo to life, and I thank you for it. Your insights into Penny's character was much needed and definitely made for a better story. Furthermore, you've been one of my best friends on this journey and I'm so glad I've gotten to know you. I enjoy our chats over Miss Piggy and Kermit's break up all the way to hashtags. You mean the world to me, and I value our friendship more than you'll ever know. Your support and belief in me makes me want to push myself in my writing. Thank you.

Batman, thank you thank you. You've been my personal cheerleader for as long as I can remember. And when I feel like giving up you are the one person I have to keep me going. Thank you for your endless humor and your lasting friendship. And as always, it's me and you 'til the end. You know what makes it special is we can go days without talking but we still pick up right where we left off.

Obi Wan Kenobi, this is it, our one shot and chance. You have inspired me so much and as soon as you are all better there's nothing you won't be able to do. I believe in you more than you will ever know. You are special, and here's knowing good things are on the way. Watch out world there's no stopping us.

The Duchess of Storms, your help in this book was a breath of fresh air and when you and Paula came together on ideas, the book took off. Together we worked the details and I value everything you've done for me. You're the one person I come to when I need a unique perspective on life. Your humor and personality are something I'm glad I get to experience.

Jacob Chance is Logan's younger brother here is the prologue and first chapter to Quake.

Written By Jacob Chance

Prologue

If you'd asked me when I was in college what I thought I would be doing in ten years' time, this wouldn't have been my answer. Life as a private investigator isn't as exciting as one might think. Sure, there are moments of danger which get my adrenaline pumping and when that happens, no other high can compare. I used to live for that feeling and for a while you could even say I was addicted to it. But the choices we make have consequences and one decision can change everything.

These days I do a lot of watching and even more waiting. I'm the guy people pay to find the truth buried under all the lies. Eventually, I see past the surface of who you're pretending to be, revealing all that you've kept hidden and I know firsthand appearances can be deceiving.

Chapter One
Kyle

Present Day

Fuck it. I can't fight the urge any longer.

I type the commands to bring up the main screen, checking to see which room she's in. I find her in the bedroom she uses, still bundled up in her comforter, just like I've imagined. I maximize her room up on the screen.

I watch her as she lowers the comforter down to her waist, before pushing it all the way to the end of the bed with her feet. Her hand slides down into the front of her panties and for a moment I think I must be imagining this.

Oh Jesus.

My heartbeat kicks up a notch and my cock goes rock hard as she tips her head back and parts her lips in pleasure. I can see her fingers slowly circling her clit through her sheer white panties and I pretend it's my hand making her gasp and twitch. Her eyes are closed in concentration, the fullness of her bottom lip is clenched between her teeth. She's absolutely focused on the overwhelming ecstasy she's experiencing.

My cock is so hard it's straining against my jeans. I undo the button and pull down my zipper, the sound it makes echoes through the silence of my office.

She trails her other hand up her stomach and tweaks her nipple.

Christ, I'm going to come in my pants if I don't get a move on. I breathe a sigh of relief when my dick is freed from my clothing. Holding it tightly in my fist, my eyes never leaving the blonde siren on my screen, I slowly stroke up and down a few times, I use my thumb, spreading the pre-come around the tip, before gripping it tighter. I move my hand faster and faster as her fingers pick up the pace and her eyes squeeze shut. She spreads her legs wide and digs her heels into the mattress and at the same time air expels from my lungs. The fingers of my free hand grip the desk so hard, my knuckles are white, while I try to fight back my release. Fuck. She's so hot. All I want to do is bury myself inside her tight, wet pussy and feel her unravel around me.

Her back arches up off the bed and her mouth opens in a soundless cry as she finds her release. Watching her is the hottest fucking thing I've ever seen. I come all over myself when my orgasm hits me quick and hard. I carefully remove my shirt, cleaning up with it, before resting my head back against the chair. While I wait for my breathing to settle down there's only one thought in my mind—I have to meet Janny Moore.

[Buy Quake for 99 cents or FREE on KU](#)

Made in the USA
Columbia, SC
11 October 2018